HOUSEBOUND

A NOVEL

BY ELIZABETH GENTRY

Lake Forest College Press
Lake Forest

First published 2013 by &NOW Books, an imprint of
Lake Forest College Press.

Carnegie Hall
Lake Forest College
555 N. Sheridan Road
Lake Forest, IL 60045

lakeforest.edu/andnow

Lake Forest College Press publishes in the broad spaces of Chicago
studies. Our imprint, &NOW Books, publishes innovative and
conceptual literature and serves as the publishing arm of the
&NOW writers' conference and organization.

ISBN: 978-0-9823156-6-8

Cover design by Jessica Berger

Book design by Jenna Brankin

Printed in the United States

For Rebecca

FOREWORD

Housebound is a multidimensional novel that moves through rooms, fields, towns, and woods as through a nightmare. The language is sensual and estranging at once. Each sentence belongs to a mind reader who intimately knows the book's many children—and former children—living and dying inside of the book. The everyday world is a real world. The everyday world might be a ghost. The deranged and delicate lyric of *Housebound* is pieced together by grammar. And if a novel is a diorama, this one is taped with very old tape, brittle and breaking—barely containing the beautiful scene. This is a terrible feat of the imagination and of a stylist's wanton, bold hand.

Reading *Housebound*, one feels trapped, searching for a way out of the danger. There is no way out, except by reading the book, of course. "You all read too much," the children are told early on in *Housebound*. This line damns us all and it's a bold statement to have early in a novel. You have to read too much to read *Housebound*—that is its beauty and terror.

Indeed, the language swirls—breathy and careful—like a child you love whispering too close to your ear. It is too much but you love it. It doesn't feel very good but you love it. The hot words hang there, and in part you love them because what they do is name everything in the world, like a child who has just learned the signs: grass spiders, glass bottles, terrible dogs, blackberry bushes, babies, piles of shoes. And as almost every child eventually learns, humans have power. People are liars. Red houses, new babies— always there. Not the danger. Yet also not quite . . . not very . . . real. How then to explain the power of things in this novel? When it is humans who so abuse power?

It cannot be explained.

In this world, nothing is right and not even the narrator will behave as a narrator should. The narrator's unruly. The gaze goes everywhere it wants to—it has a sinister and dirty direction. It stares at a girl, mostly Maggie, and moves up and down her body and up and down the paths of the town. The narration does not have desire, per se; the narrator works hard and is toiling and intense on behalf of the children—mostly of Maggie. The narrator worries about pain. Also about cupcake wrappers; everything in this novel is worrisome.

The worry is concrete; boundaries are being defined. Waking and dreaming, childhood and adulthood, daughter and mother, baby and woman, woods and town, home and house, city and country, human and dog: the binaries of a fairy tale crisscross through the novel. Constellate. And then we hesitate, because disenchantment's at work; the binaries are all muddled up—mother to husband, baby to cat, azalea to bedroom, liver to food?

The derangement is physical. The children take care of each other, but they're nearly adults—their bodies grow hair, leak fluids, have wants. Isolated, they look for safe haven in nature (flowers and water)—they walk through open doors leading to air.

The anxiety is palpable. An aesthetic completeness presides, offering little consolation but very much beauty. The unease is quite lovely; for as in a fairy tale, common sense does not operate as ought to—almost but not quite, and the not-quite is just-so. To utilize fairy-tale techniques (and there are dozens, including paradox, riddle, displacement, symmetry, lack—all wonderfully explicated by scholar Max Luthi and at work in my evolving theory of "the fairy way of reading") is to change the meaning of meaning. There is no natural law at work in the language though it follows the letter of the law quite nicely, thank you.

This strangeness produces what feels like an awakening state— one experiences it in writers as diverse as Giorgio Agamben, Emily Dickinson, Cesar Aira. And one thinks of Kathryn Davis, Katherine Mansfield, John Updike, Joy Williams: their profoundly balanced imbalance. Writers of *avant garde* fairy tales read too much and too well into the world.

In this heaven or hell, which is so remarkably life-like, so book-like, so ontologically screwed, there are "no more anecdotes, poetry recitations, ghost stories, contrived games, or late-night disclosures before the wood stove." Crime scene, children's book, family romance? *Housebound* is a horror—also a dream.

But oh! So many *surging demands* on dear Maggie, this story's main girl. She's the girl in a fairy tale—the girl trapped inside of a book. As I was once upon a time too, turning its pages.

Housebound had me spellbound.

It is such an honor to introduce Elizabeth Gentry's first novel to you.

—Kate Bernheimer

These walls enclose a world. Here is continuity spinning a web from room to room, from year to year. It is safe in this house. Here grows something energetic, concentrated, tough, serene; with its own laws and habits; something alarming, oppressive, not altogether to be trusted: nefarious perhaps. Here grows a curious plant with strong roots knotted all together: an unique specimen.

—Rosamond Lehmann,
Invitation to the Waltz

CHAPTER ONE

Leaving home felt like tunneling out of a snow that had kept everyone housebound so long they had run out of things to talk about. There were no more anecdotes, poetry recitations, ghost stories, contrived games, or late-night disclosures before the wood stove. Rather than building their knowledge of one another in successive cycles of irritation and love, memorizing each new layer as they aged and grew, the eleven members of the family had simply succumbed, once and for all, to a silence that turned them into strangers. They forgot the pressing revelations. They forgot that short surprised laugh. They forgot, too, the ring of the telephone against the wall, connecting them to people they might no longer recognize. With the radio dusty and their records scratched and worn, they perched on the ends of straight-backed chairs reading as if with peripheral vision engaged, shoulders tensed against an encroachment of space unlikely to occur. They felt suspended, always waiting for someone else to make the first move—to take a turn with the bath, to return with fresh wood, to put the pot on to boil, to summon to supper, and most of all, to grow up and to leave.

When Maggie decided to leave, the honeysuckle vines were just beginning to smother the herb garden far below her open bedroom window. Awaking in early dawn to the sound of a cough, she guessed that Douglas, the fourteen-year-old, lay without sleeping, his twin bed pushed against the wall alongside two bunks and a cradle. Presently their mother and father would pass through the nursery from their adjoining room on the far side, apparently unable to imagine that their children wanted anything more than to linger on in the great heart and heat of the room for six, the passageway to each parental entrance and exit. And why not? The oldest boys in the side rooms downstairs weren't ready to leave. The eighteen-year-old whom the children often referred to as the theologian could continue indefinitely in his independent study of philosophy and religion, since their mother ceased her instruction when each of them turned fifteen. The sixteen-year-old athlete could run half-way to the city nearly thirty miles to the west and across the railroad tracks in town straight up the ridge into mountain ravines to the east. What could such skills bring? Her brothers were delaying, preparing for nothing.

But Maggie's skill, child rearing, had been honed long ago, with the last baby now four years old. Sliding from beneath the coverlet and reaching for the lamp switch, she understood that the time had come for someone else to use this room: at nineteen, she had occupied the only private bedroom off the second-floor landing for nearly a decade. If she did not leave, perhaps no one would.

From the nightstand drawer, Maggie pulled an old favorite children's book and a new favorite novel and set them on the bed. On top of the books she placed a pocket knife with scissors, a spool of white thread stuck through with a thin needle, and an unopened pack of Teaberry gum given her by a town boy for changing the diaper of his baby sister, a small bit of contraband in a house where sweets were outlawed by their parents. Bending to reach beneath her bed, she felt for a round leather box that she had discovered on the top shelf of her closet years ago. When Maggie asked to be allowed to keep the box, her mother could not remember where they had acquired such an item—perhaps it had been in the house when they arrived, she said. Yet upon first taking the worn black handle, Maggie had imagined a raucous, gray-headed woman who drank beer and smoked cigarettes as was done in some books and perhaps on some forgotten television show, watched at someone else's house long ago. Though Maggie did not remember ever having met this low-breasted woman, she thought of her as a forgotten grandmother, one who had no trust for men or women and who steered away from babies whenever possible. Since no one spoke of relatives, the family might as well have come into being all on its own, without ancestry or extended relations, its identity gleaned from these small, oddly-shaped rooms, the steep staircase, the deep ashy swirling within the woodstove, and the thin paneling of the half-finished basement. Still, like a disgruntled fairy godmother, the imaginary grandmother had briefly appeared in the living room when, at age eleven, Maggie had been told to wait with her laboring mother until the midwife came. "I tore mine out with a coat hanger," she said with a chuckle, then faded away.

Though Maggie understood that today she would at best only accompany her father into the city to inquire about a position, she packed her clothes into the box along with the other things in case she did not return. Then she changed into a dress and pulled on a green cardigan against the spring chill. From across the hall Douglas heard the bureau drawers slide open and for no particular reason—unless because the noise was the same noise he heard every morning—became despondent: if no one left, then it was as if they all existed solely as indirect witnesses to their parents' copulation, a kind of relentless insular system in which all circled a secret central drama that only revealed itself with each new creation. Even the smallest of rustlings from the other side of the bedroom wall, noises that could have simply been the parting of his parents' bedclothes, had lately caused Douglas to awake in disgust, shamefully longing for solitude to still the early morning tides of ache. He did not consider that perhaps this four-year lapse in childbearing was final, and that whatever happened from here spun them out and away from the source, which somewhere deep had glowed warm and bright, but was now cooling, withdrawing, curling in to simply sustain itself. The unseen beginnings of change were beyond his experience or intuition, and so he had no reason to believe that there would be anything but a new cradle slid into the room in which he slept with the twelve-year-old whose baby fat was gathering at her chest, the eleven-year-old who kicked the mattress while she slept, the ten-year-old who pressed his cheek to the window each morning to stare at the gravel driveway below, the eight-year-old who bounced a ball against doors to pass the time, and the four-year-old who for attention still tried to slip into self-conscious baby talk until everyone stiffened and looked away, embarrassed for him.

And so it was that Douglas, along with all of the other children, felt some strange new contraction in the heart when the family had settled onto the benches of the long wooden table for breakfast, where Maggie made her announcement.

"There haven't been any babies here for quite some time," she said, her voice deep and almost hollow. She nodded toward Bertie, the four-year-old, sitting on the middle sister's lap to get closer to his hot cereal. Bertie looked up from beneath blond hair as if he had been caught growing up and was responsible for no longer charming them. "I don't want any babies of my own," she continued, "so it's time for me to find some work to do."

Some time had passed since two complete sentences had been spoken over breakfast that did not pertain to some practical task— an instruction or bid for help. The children shifted on the benches, unable to believe they were witnessing a declaration of intent that even their parents' refusal could not erase: Maggie had not asked for permission nor had she made the announcement in private. She made it in front of all of them deliberately, suggesting that they, too, might seek out something else.

But their father did not resist. Maggie half-expected her parents to make some other suggestion, to promote an idea of their own. Perhaps in taking the initiative she would trigger memory of the dreams they had once harbored for their children when they decided to educate them beyond the limited capacity of the rural public schools. Instead, her father looked just past her, through the kitchen and toward the back door, the broken red veins visible in his cheeks and nose, one wisp of hair lying across the top of his head. "There are always babies in the city," he said. "And some people I know." He speared egg with his fork, signaling that they might all resume eating.

Their mother never looked up. She took the littlest from his sister's lap and put him on her own, tucking her long brown hair behind one ear as she did so. "He's spilling," she said, the unsolicited explanation the only sign that she resented this disruption. In that one phrase, they all knew that in Maggie's absence, their mother would redouble her efforts at caring for Bertie, who was furthest from leaving her, a safe investment. Bertie suddenly felt restless and cramped, as if he were growing bigger in his mother's lap, and her thighs no longer cushioned him.

Knowing her father would want to leave promptly in order to reach the government finance office in time for Monday morning work, Maggie left the table after quickly finishing her breakfast. She did not wait, as on every day, for the others to finish. She took a last bite of potato and without a word placed her fork across her plate and mounted the steep stairs to her bedroom. This seamless motion was like a soaring in her mind and in the minds of her siblings—fork to plate, heel to floor, toe to first wooden stair, the lift and swing of her denim dress over her boots. She would not be asked to resume her seat at the table, they knew, not now or ever. They turned from the sight of her retreating hemline back to their half-empty plates.

* * * *

The new order—that Maggie would no longer join them at table— was in place that very evening, when she and her father returned home from the city, having found her a position in a daycare center that would begin in three days. Edwin, the eight-year-old throwing his battered orange ball against the barn door when they arrived home, was so surprised at the slamming of two car doors instead of one that he missed his ball and had to chase it across the grass. Maggie never once looked in his direction. She appeared disoriented, as if she had run through the woods believing that she was being chased by a wolf, only to be stopped by someone who told her there had never been a wolf. Grasping the ball between his fingertips again, Edwin felt shamed somehow, caught doing something routine when she had ventured out to something new.

After a moment he followed her to the kitchen, where she slumped alone on the stool drinking a glass of milk, the heels of her low boots slung over the bottom rail, her knees splayed beneath her skirt. When the screen door closed behind him, Maggie looked up from beneath heavy dark bangs with a small smile.

"I saw a toy shop full of balls in the city today," she whispered, as if she were afraid their mother would hear. He fingered the dusty basketball in his hands without speaking, such an exchange having never been demanded of him before. "There were other toys, too, but mostly balls. All different sizes and colors." She looked away, remembering. His knowledge of the rest of the world, like hers, came from library books and from what the town kids said, at least before today, and so with her he now imagined not only the toy store, but a bookstore run by two young women who lived together in an apartment above the shop; an antique store owned by an old man who scowled when someone's entrance tripped the doorbell; a fabric store, boring except for one bolt in the window—deep blue with gold edging that folded stiff and crisp. Perhaps as she gazed into her milk glass his sister was deciding that book knowledge was enough. But as Edwin passed Maggie without a word to disappear into the living room, he thought that reading offered merely a glimpse—not nearly enough at all.

She would miss him when she left, Maggie thought, watching her little brother retreat. She might even miss the rest of them, a somber mass with little concern for her coupled with profound expectations that pulled and tugged. This morning she and her father had spent the half-hour drive into the city in silence. She watched as the familiar streets and houses dropped away after the first curvy mile, followed by the grocer and farmers' market and library and the other places in town where the family walked. Just beyond the railroad tracks they passed the courthouse, then the public health department, then an old gas station. There the mountains fell away and the car reached the flat stretch of highway that their father would have them believe he endured every morning and evening for their sake.

When the five or six tall buildings of the city sparkled against the sky long before she expected them to, Maggie was embarrassed to realize that their father did not just retreat from their consciousness every day when he left, the way that characters did when the children set down their books for a break. Minutes later, watching the people move within the shadows created by buildings, she believed she'd guessed her father's secret: he deliberately kept this place to himself, speaking of it only as a sinister and dirty destination at the end of a long and arduous journey. Certainly many of the windows were boarded up, and a mass of forlorn figures hovered at the entrance to a large public library. Still, she had also seen a bookstore with pale blue curtains, a greening park with a fountain, a stone statue of a hunched bear, and a man selling flowers on the corner. She did not know why her father would wish to mislead them about the city, except to hoard the power that came from moving easily among strangers, an ability she could sense in him even as he pulled the brown station wagon into the parking garage. As for her, she shrank back from the unfamiliar faces.

Her father left her in the bakery near the offices where he worked so that he could make inquiries discreetly, without parading her around like an orphan or a prostitute he said, the only thing he had said yet. He bought her a coffee, making it acceptable for her to spend the morning in the shop, and since she had never had any and he had set it down so formally before her on the small table, without offering either cream or sugar, she could not tell whether he was welcoming her to his world or telling her she'd be sorry she'd come. Only a little while later, when the coffee caused her to feel a slow rising panic and a need to move about that she could not indulge, did she decide that it was the latter.

Draining the last of the milk as she had the coffee, Maggie recalled that tonight was her night to prepare dinner for the rest of them. She slid off the stool and placed the empty glass in the bottom of the sink, where she hesitated over her mother's low murmur, reading quietly to Bertie in the living room as if he were ill. Outside a jump rope snapped, and from the other side of the pantry wall, Warren coughed. Her family was not caught up in their routine activities, oblivious to her return. Instead they were lingering over them in hopes that she would step in to prepare the meal, as if this morning's conversation had never occurred. If she did this for a number of days, they might decide that she had changed her mind about leaving, as it was in some ways inconvenient and troubling for them, and eventually allow her to return to table. Tonight their father would announce that Maggie was leaving for work at the end of the week, yet the rest of the family would wait to see whether she would really go, as her failure to do so would explain something about themselves and something about what the world had to offer. What they could assume or hope for. What they hoped for now was calm and a good meal; she was a better cook than her mother or brothers.

Maggie opened the refrigerator to seek out ingredients for a recipe or the rare available snack in a household that ate only regulated meals. When she did so, she heard faint laughter through the screen door. Her sisters were somewhere beyond the meadow. They were not waiting on her to make dinner at all—they had likely forgotten her. Maggie recognized a faint hint of Agnes' authoritative storytelling voice, the lilt and inflection summoning her from the kitchen. Taking three long carrots and a bruised apple from the bottom drawer of the refrigerator, she let the screen door fall closed behind her: she would not be humbled by service to a family that wanted to let her know they had already forgotten her at the same time that they willed her back in her place.

At the edge of the yard, Maggie stuffed the food in the pockets of her dress and left through the gate, a standalone iron archway that her mother had years ago positioned in what was now a gap between the hedges. When she first placed the ornament in the yard, back when she still had some desire to shape and adorn their surroundings, the bushes had not yet been planted: the archway stood on its own, granting entrance or exit to nowhere that couldn't be reached simply by stepping over the grass, as if their mother had wanted to rip a hole in space that would allow entrance to another world. Then the fast-growing bushes were planted, and the vines slowly crept up both the archway and the bushes, ivy twisting around the iron bars. Douglas, who had begun to demonstrate an interest in yard work over the past year, would eventually clear the vines and trim the hedges. Last fall he had also cut a path through the overgrown meadow sloping down into the woods, just past the raised bed where their mother had once kept a vegetable garden. Though this path would not last much longer in the warm weather, Maggie used it now to walk through the knee-high grasses.

At the tree line, she came upon her sisters, sitting side-by-side on the horizontal leg of a grapevine with their skirts tucked beneath them, chatting and eating mulberries from their stained palms. They grew quiet as she approached. The eleven-year-old stared wide-eyed from beneath the sharp center part of her long gold hair, but Agnes sniffed and looked away.

"We had a sister like you once," Agnes said with a scowl, green eyes darting back to Maggie and then away again. Maggie was startled by the boldness of the rebuke.

"Is she a ghost?" Ellen whispered in her sister's ear.

"Are you a ghost?" Agnes asked, smoothing the brown ponytail that rested across her shoulder. "Ellen would like to know."

Maggie hesitated. She did not know what she could say to them of her leaving. She had not comforted the girls in some time, and only then when they had cried over a stubbed toe or a bee sting. Neither girl was now crying, and neither would ask about her trip to the city today, or about what was to come, so she could not think of how to bring it up. "Where did you get the mulberries?" Maggie said.

"Ghosts don't eat," Ellen said, blue eyes gazing directly at Maggie. Then she pointed to the tree a few feet away, branches low enough to reach.

Maggie turned, remembering. She hadn't picked from the mulberry tree since her mother gave birth to Edwin, shortly before the big snow that buried everything in the woods for days. Not long after, Maggie had gotten her first period, becoming an unwilling participant in a cycle she could not control that was linked to the space torn from between her mother's legs, as if the universe was not one whole piece but could be altered to suddenly offer more, the way the archway, once placed, suggested an entrance that had not otherwise existed. On asking about the health of the mother and baby, the neighbors in town referred to the birthing as natural, as it had been done at home, though to Maggie there could not have been anything less natural. Her mother had complained that the baby would not take her nipple, which also seemed unnatural. Why not let it die if it had so few instincts? The last time Maggie entered the woods, as her mother tried to nurse inside, everything turned grotesque: the vines that consumed all other vegetation, the bright yellow lichen on a log, the yellow jacket eating a dead wasp, the white unripe berries of the mulberry tree like insect larvae. Worse, when she returned to the house, she could find no rest: centipedes surfaced on the wood floors by the dozens to be captured by the spider webs flourishing in every corner. Mice scratched in the walls. And once she sprinkled dried dill onto the fried eggs she was making for her family only to notice that the thin green slivers moved against the whites, the herb infested with some kind of worm. She had longed for winter so everything would freeze and die.

In spite of this aversion to the natural world, Maggie, too, had been pulled into slavery to potential procreation at twelve, when without warning she endured two days with a relentless hunger while clear fluid dripped persistently from between her legs. Two weeks later she experienced rage and deep sadness, an excruciating intolerance to noise, spasms of pain in her back, and the week-long monitoring of the useless blood draining from her body. This routine, she found, would occur at regular intervals, again and again, causing a notable percentage of her time to be occupied by forces she could not see, the symptoms of which she was always turning toward just as soon as she thought she had turned away. Her mother showed her how to fold and then wash the rags, which they used in place of the napkins the grocer sold in order to keep expenses down. She did not offer words of celebration or consolation. "Just another form of diaper," her mother said, and went back to her newest child.

From then on, Maggie began having nightmares in which she was genuinely at a loss as to how she had become pregnant. In waking life she understood all too well how babies came to be, but in the dreams, she was always vaguely suspicious that some sibling or parent caused the problem by pressing particularly close with unspoken thoughts and ingrained habits—a distinct form of chewing or a suppressed belch.

Now Maggie saw that the mulberries were not quite ripe. She tore one from its stem, popped it into her mouth, then spit out the sour pulp a moment later. She tried once more before coming back to the grapevine, where her sisters were licking their fingers as if they had feasted on a bushel.

"What story were you telling earlier?" Maggie asked, hoping to make conversation.

Agnes frowned. "What do you mean?"

"Earlier, from the house, I heard you telling a story. What was it about?"

"I don't know," she said flippantly.

"Of course you do," Ellen said to Agnes. Then to Maggie, "She was retelling the story that she's been reading aloud to us in bed at night. About a boy who lives in a cave."

Agnes rolled her eyes. "Oh, that story."

"Except that in the told version," Ellen said. "It's about us. That way we get to hear a story about ourselves."

"That sounds nice," Maggie said, and indeed she thought it was.

"You could do it, too," Ellen said, giving a little kick. The grapevine shook. "You could tell us one now, about ourselves." Ellen leaned hopefully toward Maggie. "A real one."

"You shouldn't ask her that, Ellen," Agnes hissed.

"We're in the woods," Ellen said, "And so it's not against the rules."

"It's not against the rules in any case," Maggie said, though since no story rose readily to her lips, she wondered if her sisters had a better grasp of how things worked than she did. Surely she had at one time told them stories? She thought for a moment, as Ellen stared hopefully and Agnes twisted the cloth tie of her dress around one finger. Maggie could recall the smell of the wild mint they used to chew, the heat radiating from the hair she braided in the sunny backyard, the hiccups erupting from Ellen's small body, the sour expression on Agnes' face when she ate cabbage. Maggie could feel again her movements in caring for them, stooping and lifting, wiping and changing, carrying and chasing. All of these motions imbedded the girls in her memory. But they had asked for a story—a linked chain of events that indicated something about who they were or what they could become—not a catalogue of the senses. She opened her mouth to speak, then closed it again.

"I told you she couldn't do it," Agnes said.

"But she's the only one who would be willing," Ellen said, biting her bottom lip.

"I'll have to think a little," Maggie said lamely. If she told them they often smelled like the ginger they helped her to peel in the kitchen, they would be disappointed.

"Won't you be eating with us tonight?" Agnes said, free to taunt now that Maggie had failed them.

"She'll be eating in the woods, silly," Ellen said, appearing to have recovered from the tears that threatened just a moment before. She pointed to Maggie's bulging pockets. "When the house doesn't want you, the woods won't complain."

"But Maggie hates the woods," Agnes said, scrutinizing her older sister, "so she must be on her way to the fat lady's house."

"Where?" Maggie asked.

"You know, the fat lady neighbor." Agnes waited for recognition from her sister, and when none came, sighed and pointed toward the cane break beyond the fence. "Don't you know? Little Sis and I used to go there. She would give us cupcakes. They tasted good and were decorated nicely."

"We've not been back in a while," Ellen said, wistfully.

"We didn't always like going," Agnes reminded Ellen.

Ellen nodded, then said to Maggie, "She'll laugh on your knees, which is sometimes quite funny, but also a little uncomfortable. Her breath is hot and her teeth are sharp."

Agnes' pale brow knit tight. "And she keeps a prowling man. We didn't like him."

"What's worse," Ellen said, "sometimes she sits on you. It's quite scary to be sat upon by a fat lady."

Indeed, Maggie could suddenly envision a round woman who

had every type of metal frosting tip to decorate the tops of her cakes, though she did not seem in memory like a real woman, but like someone from a book she had read as a child—perhaps her sisters had been reading the same book. She recollected then that her role in relation to her sisters was maternal, authoritarian. "You all read too much," she chided. She did not actually believe it was possible to read too much, but she did not know what to say to them unless she was asking a question, giving an instruction, or delivering a reprimand. She might not even have entertained the notion of excessive reading at all if the town children as well as the librarian herself had not said something to this effect on more than one occasion. "Besides," she said, "we're not supposed to leave our property. You know that father doesn't like us to trespass."

In response, her sisters stared at her blankly, as if she had just said something in an unknown language. Then they both laughed.

"Well, it's better to eat out here, really," Ellen said, hopping off the vine. It swung back then came forward with a jarring motion. "The table won't let you speak."

"Hey now!" Agnes protested the rough dismount, grabbing hold of the vine to keep her balance.

"She broke the rule this morning, and spoke over breakfast," Ellen said to Agnes, as if she'd been misunderstood.

"There's no rule, honey pot. You've made it up."

"Of course there's a rule." Ellen turned back to Maggie. "Big Sis and I have been thinking of breaking it for some time. We haven't because we didn't know what might happen to us."

Agnes slid from the vine daintily. "Now we know," she said.

"Yes, now we know—if you speak in a certain way, saying certain things, you can't come back."

"That punishment wouldn't apply in all cases," Agnes said. "You're exaggerating."

"I might have said to Sis, 'I see your breast buds!'" The youngest reached out and pinched her sister's small breast, who screamed, then burst into giggles.

"They're mine!" she said in triumph. "Get your own." They grabbed hands and took off running up the path through the meadow, as if, Maggie thought, they were being chased by a wolf. They looked over their shoulders to see whether she would follow, or perhaps to see whether she would simply drift away, like a good ghost. Maggie, shivering with the coming dusk, turned to look into the woods behind her. In the dim gray light, the rotting hackberry trees sagged with the weight of the grape vines, and the gaping tunnels of grass spiders shimmered beneath the choke of privet.

CHAPTER TWO

Climbing the stairs, Quinn squeezed quietly by his father, who looked past him as he often did, his mind on other matters. But Quinn wasn't fooled. Whatever there was down that road their father traveled, it was more than he let on and at the same time wasn't much at all.

From the window on the landing, Quinn spotted Maggie in the backyard, just as his two sisters had told him he would. She was sitting on a grapevine at the far end of the meadow, staring across the fence toward the cane brake with her face in profile. He blinked and rubbed his eyes, swollen from crying. He hadn't expected her to return today, but he did not believe she could be a ghost, as his sisters had teased. She was more likely to be an angel, gently cupping the back of his head with one hand if he were in her way and she needed to move past. His mother had long ago retreated into some place of her own that did not invite others, but his oldest sister had not ignored him when Edwin and Bertie came along.

When Maggie remained seated, Quinn understood that she'd been sent to stand at the edge of the woods as punishment, as he had been some years ago after pinching Edwin very hard on the arm. That day, his father had required him to keep his back to the forest and stare at the house, where all of the windows stared blankly back at him. He stood there sweating from the August heat and from fear, unable to hear whether someone or something was approaching from behind because of the insects swarming in the trees. He expected Ellen or Agnes to comfort him by appearing at the landing window, but when this did not occur he realized they were all going about their usual activities, disregarding him, forgetting him as if something had already snatched him into the forest never to return. No one really believed him when he said that tramps from the train tracks sometimes came through the woods and down to the trickle of creek, but he had found their empty, strong-smelling bottles, a knife, and once, an old woolen blanket.

Which was why he put his hand against the glass now, signaling support to Maggie in spite of his worry that there might be repercussions for aligning himself with her. In a book he had read recently, wild dogs were said to sometimes collect other neighborhood dogs left free to roam by their owners, and when they did this, the kindest of pets became part of an aggressive gang, following the leader who would choose some weaker prey to kill for no reason except that weakness inspired scorn and loathing. If Quinn were ever in a pack of terrible dogs, he knew that even though he would not want to participate in violence, he would still remain part of the group, not so much because he was afraid of becoming the victim, but because leaving would cause so much pain that he wondered how anyone ever managed it.

When his runner brother summoned them all to supper, Quinn hesitated, knowing that he would now need to leave Maggie in the growing dark. In his delay, he saw her slide off the grapevine and begin walking in the direction of the creek, as if giving him permission to leave. He was afraid for her, abandoning her punishment, out in the dusk with the tramps. He was also afraid of how the table might seem without her, which is what he assumed everyone else was afraid of, since they were eating later than usual. But when he arrived at the bottom of the stairs a moment later, he remembered that tonight was Maggie's night to cook for them. Since she had not done so, Phillip had come in early from jumping rope to cut up radishes and cheese and yesterday's bread and pull the last of the meat from Sunday's cooked chickens, a cold supper that closely resembled lunch.

Because the long benches allowed the family to spread out, Maggie's place was neither empty nor occupied. As the eldest now, Warren simply slid farther down to compensate. He was now positioned not quite directly across from his father, his thick shoulders slumped forward with this responsibility. Taking his place at the other end of the table beside Agnes, Quinn could see that Warren was working problems out in his head and would not concern himself over Maggie's absence. The slightest tremor in Phillip's thin fingers, however, suggested that he felt put upon by Maggie's failure to feed them. This tremor, captured in a deliberate effort to pull apart the stale bread, assumed the others would share and indulge his sense of inconvenience. Quinn, too, began to feel the injustice in the cold gel around the base of his chicken leg.

They all understood that this small hint of resentment that Phillip had been allowed to express was what led their father to turn to Douglas across the table and say, "You'll want to go ahead and move into the open room."

Douglas nodded, the freckles on his cheeks fading into a pink flush.

Then to Phillip, their father said, "And if you'll put the cradle in the basement. Bertie's more than old enough to sleep in a bed now."

Their mother shifted on the bench, aggrieved that her husband was removing her youngest son's last token of infancy, the oversized wooden crib that, admittedly, his limbs had been tucked into a little too tightly for a while now. She felt a surge of panic: there would be no more babies.

Of herself and her sister, Agnes said, "We'll make up the hall bench." Maggie had failed to tell them a story, after all, and so she would have to sleep on the cushioned wooden chest on the upstairs landing with her legs hanging off one end, just as anyone in the nursery would have to do if sick, quarantined from the others. Maggie had also taken the last of the apples without leaving the stem that the two sisters lately collected to play princess and the pea, hiding stems and kernels of corn beneath the mattresses of their brothers to see who spent a sleepless night tossing and turning. They had enjoyed remarkable results with Douglas, whose darkly-ringed eyes suggested that he never slept at all, though as they were both such good sleepers themselves, they could not be entirely sure. Now they could test Maggie, punishing her even more than sleeping on the bench would punish her, as surely as they had a right to do, left with so many men and one absent-minded woman, without protection.

* * * *

Maggie, climbing the split rail fence of their property, knew that some petty form of revenge was likely being enacted in her absence from dinner, and felt a surge of gratitude that she would soon be out of reach of retribution. Years ago she'd been disciplined for climbing to the top of the cast iron gate in order to see out over the trees, and for sliding over the frozen water beneath the culvert in the road; the culvert, her mother said, was where dangerous men and sometimes wild animals liked to warm themselves in winter. At Quinn's age, she had been disciplined for sinking her fingernails deep into her younger brother's arm in a rage, the source of which she could not recall. Always the punishment was the same: her mother would not speak to her. Sometimes for a few hours, sometimes a day. Perhaps then the family's overall habit of silence had not grown from familiarity at all, but from the repeated and cumulative punishments of nine children over the course of nearly twenty years. Now that the youngest, too, was finally learning how he was expected to behave, they might have felt some renewed interest in communication, had not Maggie begun the day by signaling her departure.

In a couple of hours her family would retire, at which time she might return to the house with little self-consciousness or shame. In the meantime, there seemed no great harm in breaking one more rule by wandering away from their property. She felt drawn downhill, toward the stand of river cane with its tall stalks and thin, fluttering leaves. Through a single gap in the cane that she supposed the children helped to maintain, Maggie soon reached the creek, a shallow seeping of water that parted the long grasses. A neat row of rocks led across.

Before she crossed, Maggie hesitated, believing for a moment that she heard a sound like the faint roll of wheels over stone, which within the instant that she attempted to identify it, transformed into the sound of sap snapping in burning firewood. Glancing around for the source of the sound, she heard a high-pitched squeal like a woman in pain that turned into the whistle of the evening train, the only sound that distinguished itself and then won out over the others as the train passed through town a mile away. In waiting for the shrillness to release her, Maggie chided herself for being so uneasy about a place where her younger siblings no doubt played regularly, pulling against the tether of the house. She scanned the tree line on the far bank, then felt for sure footing on the mossy stones.

On the other side of the creek, the path twisted through a series of blackberry bushes in bloom, then climbed a short rise that appeared to give way to a grassy knoll. Just before stepping into the open, Maggie envisioned a two-story house with peeling white paint. Upon entering the clearing a moment later, she felt unsurprised to discover a two-story house with peeling white paint. Overgrown holly bushes loomed on each side of the front porch. The house was like something she had read about in a book, both threatening and inviting, strange and familiar. She glanced in the direction of her own house, which the cane brake now hid, then took a step into the yard filled with shoulder-high weeds. In the middle of the lawn sat a rusty push mower, which someone had used to create a passage from the front porch to the gravel driveway at the right of the house, where an old gray sedan hunched in the grass. The road beyond the house quickly disappeared into the tree line.

Maggie was on the verge of turning around when the front door opened and a bald, bulky man stepped onto the porch to scrutinize her. She hesitated, remembering her sisters' reference to a prowling man and a fat lady. Before she spoke, however, a woman's voice called from deep within, as if the house itself was asking from its rocky foundation, "Who's there?" The man did not reply, but simply waited in the doorway. From politeness Maggie felt compelled to take a step or two forward, as if to answer for herself. The smell of sugar and chocolate wafted from inside. Then the question came again, closer now.

"I don't know," the man in the doorway finally called back gruffly. "But she's like a long-legged colt."

Maggie felt the inappropriateness of his remark and turned to go without a word. At the edge of the yard, she heard the woman's voice from behind her.

"Margaret? Is that you?"

Maggie turned to see a very wide woman with a thick black bun and large round glasses emerge from the shadows. She was holding a white plastic tube tipped with metal and appeared slightly distracted.

"You should come inside," she said, wiping one hand on a full red apron with white ruffles, "but just for a little while. The tramps roam the woods at night."

Maggie thought only Quinn believed in the transients who camped in the woods close to the train. When the man stepped back from the doorway, she hesitated one moment more before following the woman into the house. They entered a room to the right, which was laid with an ill-fitting carpet so thick and wrinkled that she wobbled when she walked across it. Against one wall, a sagging couch was covered with recipe books and whisks and metal mixing bowls. In the second room, white cake boxes cluttered a wooden table.

"You know me?" Maggie said as they slowly circled through the otherwise empty rooms toward the back of the house, passing a small bare kitchen.

"Well, of course," the fat lady replied without looking back. "You've changed well enough, though, after ten years or more. Taller and skinnier."

"Like a long-legged colt," the man's voice echoed above them. The two women had arrived at the base of a set of stairs leading to the second floor. At the top of the stairs the man's bare heel was just disappearing behind a doorway.

"Shut up, you old pervert!" the fat woman yelled. Maggie looked at the other rooms beyond the woman and realized that the first floor of the house was built in a circle with the stairway in the center. The man had taken the other direction and come out in front. "You'll like the attic well enough when you're stuck there," the woman grumbled. She handed Maggie the tube of frosting, then reached down to the base of the stairs to grasp a loop of coiled rope. With a huge groan, she seized the strap and lifted the staircase, which came up as a unit. When she had it raised above her head, she fitted the loop over a hook and took a long wooden staff that was leaning against the wall and propped it under the first stair.

Beneath them a new set of stairs lead down into the basement, where the scent of sugar hung heavy in the air. At the bottom, they arrived in a subterranean kitchen lit brightly with fluorescent bulbs, as if it were a laboratory, though for a moment Maggie had a vision of the room that this one had replaced, a dark workshop illuminated by a parrot lamp and littered with colored glass like a pirate's cave. Now, however, the walls were white and lined with white cabinets, a double sink, and a large oven. Concrete stairs ascending to the yard were visible through the window of a closed door. At the center of the room, a high wooden table served as an island, where a chocolate cake with red flowers awaited the further attentions of its maker.

"You can sit there," the fat lady said, pointing to a tall counter stool. Remembering her sisters' warnings, Maggie noted that the stool was too high for the woman to be able to sit on her, though her knees were still very prominent, feet tucked beneath her on the top bar of the stool. She had discovered today just how playful her sisters could be, however, which might also mean that they were simply liars. Besides, the fat lady might only laugh on your knee if you were very young, assuming that she was amusing you.

Since Maggie was clearly known to her hostess, she was afraid to insult her by asking for her name, which the fat lady did not think to give on her own. Instead, the woman simply went to the refrigerator and pulled out a cupcake with white frosting and sliced strawberries on top, handing it to Maggie. "Strawberry," she said. "A favorite of yours, if I recall."

"Thank you," Maggie said. She hesitated a moment, remembering her household's prohibition against sugar, then began to peel back the wrapper. "You know my sisters, too?" she said, as the woman returned to her icing.

"Of course. Though it's been a number of months since their last visit. It's the same with all of you, from your family. The reading family, swallowed by your stories. Your older brothers I also no longer see."

Maggie was perplexed. For years now, the only neighbors she visited with were the ones who lived along the road toward town and who exchanged polite words with the family on their weekly trip to the library. "And the little ones?" she asked. "Do they come?"

"Edwin comes sometimes. Not the ten-year-old he tells me about. Nor the smallest."

"Oh," Maggie hesitated. "My father?"

"Never your father, or not for a very long while anyway." The woman paused, pushing her glasses back onto the bridge of her nose. "We've got a thing about fathers around here. We don't much like them."

"You mean you and the man who answered the door?"

"Me and my own daughter, who, like you, is grown, but comes to visit. The man upstairs is a necessity. He replaced my husband. My husband, in any case, was paralyzed on one side. He walked with a cane. And so he wasn't as much good to me as I thought he might be and in many ways was very bad. But the paint must be scraped and the cakes delivered. And the man upstairs is no father in any case, of mine or anyone else's children."

Maggie wondered how long the man upstairs had been there, given that she had not seen any evidence of scraped paint. Still, she had no particular reason to be bothered by the woman's views on fathers, having only really noticed her own father today, the one day she had seen him do something besides read the newspaper or roam the property repairing fences. What she saw was that he was something of a heartless man, leaving her in the coffee shop all morning with the surging demands of the caffeine, but that he also might prove to be an insignificant one, now that she would not be living with him, abiding by his rules.

"I've been to the city today," Maggie said, "but on the whole we've been rather housebound for quite some time." She hoped in this way to offer some explanation for her long absence, in case she had hurt the woman's feelings. As she spoke, she wondered if being housebound were an entirely natural phenomenon, since the fat lady seemed to believe her family's behavior was unusual. There had been that big spring snow one year—how many years ago now? A decade perhaps—that kept them in far longer than their usual snows. Even their father had remained home from work, making the weather seem a kind of holiday at first, though their mother still taught them lessons between nursing the newest baby. But then the snow had remained for days, and they had all grown bored with it—with the tunnel that Warren dug in the garden and with the books that they could not exchange at the library and with watching the road for the brightly colored scarves of the kids from town who at that time still came to play.

They had grown quiet under the weight of the snow. They had grown uncomfortable with the presence of their father, who was not usually around so much and who expected things of them that were not clearly defined, having to do with how organized, efficient, or active they were. He became restless, with much in the way of excess movement from him, clomping to the barn in his boots, to the basement in his boots, up the stairs in his boots, as he covered windows with plastic and stuffed towels into holes and put to rights an already ordered supply of canned goods in the basement and pantry, then disappeared for long spells to shovel and check the fences. Upon her husband's return from these excursions, their mother looked up briefly and intently, as if she blamed the storm on him and wondered what they had all done to merit this kind of punishment. Perhaps then the weather had been the problem, the familiarity cultivated within the enclosed space growing into a silence that did not thaw when the eaves began dripping a few days later. Though the weather changed, nothing changed inside the house. Their father went back to work. They used less wood.

The woman executed a particularly intricate rose, then said, "If you went to the city, you must be preparing to leave."

"Yes," Maggie said with pride, unexpectedly grateful to be able to make this announcement. "I'm to take care of babies for a daycare center."

"There's always babies."

"That's what my father said."

The woman looked up sharply from the rose, her eyes hidden behind the reflection of the florescent bulbs against her glasses. "I thought I made it clear we're not big on fathers around here."

Startled, Maggie quickly apologized. She had paid too little attention and missed the household rule. She searched for a place to begin again, to indicate that she had accepted the reproof without offense. "I met the director, who introduced me to the other women." The administrator of the large church that housed the daycare had valued that she dressed plainly, listened attentively, and spoke rarely, as her father informed her on their drive home. The director cared, too, that the timing of her father's inquiry to a fellow government employee came the day after the old woman who had previously been caring for the babies was buried, with a substitute hired only for the week. This much Maggie gathered from the director herself, who wore pink lipstick and high heels and gave her a tour of the dusty old building, with its stone arches, tall windows covered in red velvet curtains, and a worn grand piano that anyone could play, things Maggie tried to describe to the fat lady now. The church, she said, offered ministries to the poor and a senior center and a daycare, with one small room on the second floor that was to be Maggie's, where a single bed covered with a quilt was pushed against a wall next to a nightstand. Maggie would share the bathroom down the hall with other female live-in staff, working in exchange for meals and an allowance.

What Maggie did not say was that in the dining room where she had shared lunch with the staff, she could see that the other employees were skeptical of her. The women who took care of housekeeping and food service and the senior center were all gleaned from the church's rescue mission. Their hands were rough from the chlorine they used to clean with and their gums were dark and receding from tobacco. When Maggie entered the room, they looked pointedly away. She had approached the fold-out tables with an odd measure of comfort—if she were beneath their notice, she could get her bearings slowly.

The director, however, would not allow this lapse in attention to occur for long. She smiled at Maggie, indicating with a nod that she should wait, then listened for the first crack in the conversational barricade that the other women were creating. Someone said, "Well, they could have washed the pots out, anyway," to which no one had a quick enough reply. There was a dry cough and the director spoke.

"Ladies, we should say hello to Margaret, the newest member of our staff."

They all turned to look at her as if they had not seen her arrive. The look was brief and flat and then they turned again toward their food.

"Young, ain't she?" one woman said without taking a second look, dipping a spoon into her soup with chapped red hands.

The director seemed prepared for this. She balanced her pointy chin in the heel of one hand and stared at Maggie as if she might change her mind about giving her the job. "Yes, she certainly is that," she said after a moment.

"And isn't it too soon?" one of the women who cared for the toddlers said hesitantly. "Too soon for a replacement?"

In the silence that followed, they all considered their deceased friend.

"Well, someone's got to take care of the babies, for heaven's sake," the woman next to Maggie finally said without looking up from the bread she was buttering. "No reason to get sentimental about the job."

Maggie understood that the women were imagining how quickly the work they did could be given over to someone else in the face of death or illness. They worked so hard at their tasks that it seemed no one else could do them quite as well, and yet the work needed to be done all over again as soon as it had been completed. If they left or died, someone would have to be hired right away. There would not be time for others to notice the work being undone and to miss their doing of it. Maggie saw that they felt hard toward her because she reminded them of what would happen to them all. Overwhelmed with their bitterness, she did not look down at her soft young hands and she did not smile excessively, which was how the director had no doubt eventually won them over. Instead she just looked directly at whomever was speaking, thinking that she had never been in a room full of strangers and that she could barely breathe beneath the weight of all their feelings.

"Be having a baby herself before we even get her broke in," the first woman said, and scooted back her metal folding chair.

"Hush now," the director said gently. "She's helped birth and raise eight siblings out in the country. I think she knows a little something about babies," and here she turned and let her gaze linger on Maggie, "and that includes how not to have one herself."

This last comment had reassured Maggie that she and the director would have some point of agreement. The church formed an entire world that she would rarely need to leave, something Maggie understood.

"I'm to start on Friday," Maggie now said to the fat lady, though with the dreamy sweetness of the cupcake, she felt as if she might never have to go anywhere again at all.

"Good—no reason to be slow about it," the woman said in a congenial tone. "I've been trying to leave this place for years, and yet I rarely get beyond the front door. Going must be done quick and clean." She eased up on the last flower. "That is, if it's to be done at all." She looked at Maggie and gave a half smile. "Which reminds me. You'll need to head on now."

"Your cake looks lovely," Maggie said, sliding off the stool. "Do you sell them?"

"I used to deliver them to the grocer in town," the woman said, turning to the sink to rinse her hands. "Before my ex-husband's reputation ruined that for good. Now I sell them only sometimes, to some people. I give them to the man," she pointed toward the ceiling with one dripping wet finger, "sometimes just to eat, and sometimes to sell for supplies." Drying her hands on a towel, she said, "You'll see yourself out now."

Maggie thanked her for the cupcake and at the top of the stairs turned left instead of right, circling back in the direction that the prowling man had come earlier. Against one wall a fireplace loomed cold and unused, the heat for the house now coming from wide vents in the floor. The carpet here was also thick and mislaid, with only a few scattered pieces of furniture in the second of the two rooms—an armchair and a lawn chair and a tall wooden table lamp sitting on the floor next to a television. Maggie pictured her sisters crowded in front of the cartoons that the town kids who had televisions talked about, giggling over the funny parts, eating pink frosting roses from wax paper. Unsure whether she was relying on memory or imagination, she could envision her younger self here, too, relieved to have escaped from her brothers and from the baby girls, glad to be talking to the fat lady about the book that she was reading, though the fat lady hadn't much cared for books even then, believing that they just created expectations for life that could not be fulfilled. Yet while Maggie did not readily recall her own memories, which were dependent upon material objects to help them take shape, she could easily conjure the stories of others learned during her lessons long ago—the great scope of histories, snippets of anecdote from inventions in science, every detail of a reread novel. The rest of her hours had been occupied by chores that did not require language for execution and that did not benefit from the dramatic possibility that story inspired. She was bound by the senses, and other skills had grown dull.

Maggie heard a chair scrape upstairs, urging her to leave. On the front lawn, stopping to allow her eyes to adjust to the dark, she turned toward the illuminated dormer window of the second floor. There the silhouette of the man stared out, pipe in his mouth, scratching his chin. Hovering in the shadows that shielded her from his view, Maggie believed that she herself must have once sat in that very window, on perhaps the only occasion she had been allowed to spend the night with the fat lady's daughter, who liked to play records and who lived in a heap of her own things, scattered and folded and crumpled in piles around the bed. But the daughter was several years older than Maggie, and so she slept the sleep of the dead as a teenager should, hours into the morning when Maggie wasn't sure whether it was polite to leave without a goodbye, whether the stairs would be properly positioned for her to descend, or whether their brooding father would be wandering around in the front yard as he sometimes did, taking a break from his work in the shop. Paralyzed by these uncertainties as well as the used, store-bought sanitary napkin that upon waking she had spotted on the floor, Maggie stared out the window in the direction of her house, hidden behind the cane, unsure whether it was better to be at one place or the other.

The man disappeared from the window just before Maggie turned toward home. Leaving the yard she passed a rotting woodpile, where she saw a glint of fuchsia and leaned forward to investigate. A whole pile of broken glass glinted in the light from upstairs—emerald, indigo, sapphire, champagne, and rose-colored shards that in some places were still held together by a thin silver-gray thread of solder. She thought again of her brief memory of the basement earlier, glittering with jewels like a dragon's hoard before being turned into a gleaming kitchen, some transformation that must have occurred after the fat lady parted ways with her husband. Afraid to linger in case the prowling man came outside, Maggie walked down the hill and crossed the creek by the rocks.

By the light of the moon Maggie climbed back over the split rail fence of her own property. From here she could see that her house was dark except for reading lamps, but by the time she cut through the meadow and opened the back door into the kitchen, everything had gone black, the downstairs windows covered in curtains that her mother shut ritualistically at the finish of each day. In the kitchen, Maggie stopped to let her eyes adjust and to listen. She took account of the state of the house, of how it had fared in her absence and in what ways it would now try to draw her in or push her out. She heard only her brother Warren clearing his throat on the other side of the pantry wall, not waiting for her, not curious about when she might return or where she had been, but simply doing what he always did. Yet she knew before she reached the first step that she would be sleeping on the landing like a sailor on watch over a calm sea, witnessing nothing, making sure nothing continued to occur. But something had already happened down beneath the depths that had only just this morning rippled to the surface, the tip of a fin that was her declaration to leave, and the whole huge leviathan would soon cause the entire ocean to heave.

CHAPTER THREE

Crouching on a mound of dirt behind the paneling in the basement, the brown rat lifted its nose to the faint smell of chicken and then something else—fruit, cheese. He had been sitting there for some time, listening to the only noises this house ever produced and no more: the scrape of a chair, the clatter of a pan, the squeak of a mattress. Someone had come and gone, breathing heavily with the awkward weight of the old cherry cradle that left the smell of spoiled milk. A month ago, when a nearby woods was cleared for planting, the rat had arrived here to the scent of garlic, onion, and butter mixed with soap and ammonia, sweat and sour clothing. Since then, however, he had been primarily subsisting off the kinds of scraps that got placed into the open air compost in the back yard, the egg shells and potato peelings. The family was thorough, boiling bones, fat, and remnant vegetables into huge pots of broth.

While he waited the light filtering through the cracks in the stone foundation faded, as did the sounds of the household settling in for sleep. Then a door opened and closed, bringing the smell of sugar and cool creek mud. The stairs squeaked, and a vibration came through the wall down to the basement before silence fell again.

When the house had been still for some time, the rat followed the new smells along the wall and up the crumbling lath, the tiny bits of plaster slipping from beneath his claws as he passed one set of baseboards and went on to a second set. Briefly he emerged at the top of an enclosed staircase that stood in the center of the house like a spine. Here, a round window spilled moonlight into a nearly forgotten room in which no human smells lingered as warning, and no sweet smells as temptation. The rat ducked again into the space between the inner and outer walls and worked his way over to the next fissure, where he slid out into the hall and along the baseboard. He took refuge beneath a wardrobe that stood in the corner of the landing. On a cushioned bench the source of the new smells now slept, her legs protruding from the end of the chest and her fingers nearly dragging the floor.

For this reason, and perhaps because of a kernel of corn tucked beneath the thin cushion stained deep with red cough syrup, Maggie was restless. In finally falling asleep in these last few minutes, she dreamt of being circled by a white unicorn. When he dipped his horned head like a charging bull, she saw that he intended to pierce her deep inside. Just as the unicorn bent to toss her into the air, the rat crept out from the wardrobe, lifted onto its hind legs, and bit into Maggie's strawberry-stained finger.

Maggie awoke to her own sharp cry in time to see the rat's thick tail disappear beneath the wardrobe. She sat up and pulled all of her limbs onto the narrow bench, trembling.

Douglas appeared at his bedroom door, his thin frame alert but wary, as if his sister might be creating a ruse to draw him out of her old room in order to steal inside and take his place. Then Quinn opened the door to the room across the hall, pushing his sandy curls away from his forehead. He hesitated in the shadows, glancing behind him, then took a step forward.

"Maggie?" he whispered tentatively. In the pale moonlight, he could only just make out her hunched silhouette.

"A rat," she whispered. She held up her little finger. In the shadows he saw that a dark stain covered her hand.

Before he could respond, their parents' bedroom door opened and closed behind him, and in an instant Maggie's father had turned on the hall light and stood glaring at her as if he, too, thought she was creating this scene so she could complain about the sleeping conditions.

"Well, what is it?" he said as he took a step toward her. Then he saw the blood and paled. He bent over, cupping his palm beneath her elbow.

"A rat," she said, pointing. "It disappeared beneath the wardrobe."

Her father glanced at the wardrobe with some alarm, then gathered the sheet from the floor beside the make-shift bed and wrapped a corner of it around the tip of her finger. Without being asked, Douglas went downstairs for a basin of soap and water, antiseptic, and bandages.

Once downstairs, Douglas groped along in the dark, nearly running into his athletic older brother, who was stumbling out of the bathroom in pajama bottoms.

"Watch out!" Douglas hissed as he might not dare under normal circumstances. "Maggie's been bit by a rat."

Phillip trained his half-closed eyes on Douglas, then yawned. He scratched the hair on his blond chest with an abandon that was never present during the day. Douglas stood beneath the foul night breath of his older brother—who was taller by half a foot at least—admiring the quantity and spread of hair that he had only rarely seen before and that gave him some sense of what he himself might look forward to what. But if he was waiting for a reaction to his dramatic news, none ever came. Phillip glanced toward the stairs, and then, as if all things above the ground floor were beyond his interest, smacked his lips and turned back to his room.

A few moments later, Douglas placed the basin of water and the soap in Maggie's lap, then stood by with iodine and a towel while she washed her finger. Their father waited with pursed lips. "We'll have to take you to the health department in the morning," he said as he released a dropper-full of medicine over the wound, "to see whether you'll need rabies shots." Quinn clutched the doorframe and fought off the tears he could not afford to show in front of his father, who already dismissed him for other tears he had shed on other days. Behind him, his two sisters stared wide-eyed from the top bunk, hidden in the shadows. They clasped hands, certain that they had been the ones to summon the rat with the kernel of corn placed under the cushion of the bench.

Then, as Agnes watched her father wrap gauze around her sister's finger, she also saw something else. She tugged at Ellen's sleeve. "Cupcake wrapper," she whispered, and the younger saw that from the top of Maggie's front breast pocket there protruded the pink ridges of one of the fat lady's cupcake wrappers. The corn kernel had not brought the rat after all. Instead, Maggie had been to see their neighbor earlier this evening after they as much as sent her there. Now if only their father wouldn't notice the cotton-candy pink.

"You'll have to sleep with your mother," their father said, standing. "In my place. I'll sleep downstairs." Maggie remained seated, astonished. She had not been in her parents' room since she was much younger. Surely the rat bite and the threat of rabies shots were punishment enough, and her father would now simply retrieve Bertie's crib from the basement, allowing her to sleep in the children's room until Friday. Instead, he waited for her to rise, glancing at her two brothers as if seeing them there for the first time. Without a word, Douglas closed himself in his room and Quinn disappeared into the shadows.

Maggie rose, entered the nursery, and closed the door behind her. Edwin was still asleep on the bunk above Bertie, who was also sleeping soundly. Her sisters were sitting up in Agnes' bunk, watching her, and Quinn stood beside the twin bed that Douglas had abandoned.

The door on the far side of the room was closed. The other children held their breath as Maggie crossed the room slowly, as if she might trip over something in the dark though there was nothing strewn about here, no toys or small stools. Reaching the other side, she gently turned the glass knob, pushed the door open a few inches, then stopped.

Watching her, the children knew there existed a dread greater than the return of the rat: sleeping with their mother, whom they had always imagined did not in fact sleep at all, but lay awake in a kind of trance, evaluating the sounds in the house and drawing conclusions that would inform interactions the following day. The siblings should have shared the burden of detecting the night noises all of these years. Instead they could only hear the hum of their mother's consciousness, somehow both sluggish and alert, which told them to carefully move about as little as possible.

Quinn came up beside Maggie, took her hand, and pulled the door closed until they heard the soft click of the latch. Sleepwalking through each day, their mother would not tell that they had disobeyed. He pointed to Ellen's empty bottom bunk.

As Maggie sat down, the light went out in the hall and they heard the creak of their father descending the stairs. Ellen waited until the sound retreated, then leaned over the edge of the bunk and said to Maggie, "You've a cupcake wrapper in the pocket of your dress." Maggie reached up and touched the crinkled paper with its tiny ridge of crumbs. "If you don't want the rat to come back, you'll have to eat it," Ellen said with remarkable authority.

Maggie thought for a moment. Making a trip downstairs to the kitchen garbage would raise the ire of their father, who was presumably settling in to sleep on the couch in the living room, where Maggie had long ago refused to sit or sleep, the cushions of the couch stained by Edwin's birthing. Their father would tell her to get back into bed immediately, to stop disturbing him. He would not necessarily have done this last week, or last year, or when she was twelve. Not until this very day would what she did create any interest for him. She felt like a life-long spy who had unwittingly blown her cover, calling attention to herself from the enemy, who was not quite ready to admit he knew who she was.

"The wrapper is mostly edible," Agnes finally whispered when Maggie hesitated, and Ellen giggled. A moment later, the two sisters had resettled themselves in their bunk and, with remarkable speed, begun breathing deeply.

Indeed, when Maggie put the wrapper in her mouth the fibrous paper that gummed against her tongue quickly dissolved into melting sugar. From across the room, Quinn almost tasted the sweetness that seemed to float on the air and felt a pang of regret that he had never visited the fat lady's house, his fear of breaking the rules and of entering the woods keeping him close to home. With his head and hands tucked tightly beneath the sheet away from the rat, he fell asleep.

Maggie remained sitting against the wall with a blanket draped over her shoulders, throbbing finger clutched to her chest. She licked her lips again, trying to scour them of any remaining traces of sugar and wondering if the scent was trapped in the heavy denim of her dress, which she had not exchanged for her nightgown. While she was in the woods, some member of the family had placed her round box at the end of the chest on the landing, as if the bench were a train station. Since they were defining the new borders of her world, she had not changed into her pajamas because it seemed senseless to do so—to descend the stairs to the bathroom where she would have privacy, to pass the night in her long cotton nightgown without privacy, then to descend the stairs again to change back into the dress that she would wear a second day before washing. She had long known that the walls of the house would yield to insects, mold, and fungus, and now she knew that rodents, too, could penetrate the boundaries. She hovered in the corner of the bottom bunk, keeping vigil for herself and the smaller children.

Downstairs on the couch in the living room, her father also lay awake, unable to sleep after the burst of adrenaline that came from seeing the blood drip from Maggie's hand. Equally unsettling was the sight of the pink cupcake wrapper sticking from her front breast pocket, proof that she had spent the evening at Mamie's house, where Maggie had not been in years. Martin could not know what it was like there now, or whether it was even a place that needed to matter, and the uncertainty caused a slow welling of sorrow and rage that he was tempted to both contain and expel, the same way he was tempted to both contain and expel Maggie, who threatened to betray him in some larger way that was difficult to identify. Unwelcome memories of the brief social interaction between the two families kept him awake most of the night. For the first time in years his two oldest boys were unable to ignore the events upstairs as part of a separate reality and had to listen instead to the springs of the couch beneath their shifting father, to the grinding of teeth in his sleep.

For their mother's part, once the unsettling cry of a child passed through her dreams and the place in the bed beside her remained unfilled, Hannah slipped from twilight into the most deep and peaceful sleep she had experienced in years.

* * * *

On their way through town the next morning, Maggie's father complained that he had not been unexpectedly late for work in twenty years, and not absent in nearly ten, when they'd all been housebound by that long snow. This morning the family had all overslept, their father ordering Maggie to slice them some bread and cheese to eat in the car, which she did clumsily, one bandaged finger extended, while he called in to work to explain the delay.

Yet when they pulled up in front of the public health department and he said, "I'll be here when you get out," he suddenly sounded diminished, as if in choosing to wait in the car he was surrendering the dominant role. He had moved to the periphery, as she saw would be more and more the case in the future. He would squint into the sunshine as he waited, sweating in the heat beneath the windshield, growing bored in his solitude.

A moment later, Maggie tugged on the heavy front door, which opened onto a lobby filled with people reading newspapers or bouncing babies on their knees. She recognized the red plastic scoop chairs from when she had come here for vaccinations as a child.

From behind a clear plastic partition off to one side, a receptionist waved. "Well hello there," she called warmly. When Maggie approached the counter, the woman beamed at her. "You always did have the most beautiful dark hair!"

Maggie leaned toward the half-moon cut into the plastic. "Do I know you?" she said.

The woman's smile wilted a little. "It's true then that I've aged tremendously." She touched a lock of the blond hair that fell to her shoulders. "The other girls who work here always refuse to tell me the truth, but then, they've seen me week after week for the past ten years. How could they be good judges?"

"I doubt you've aged at all," Maggie said. After all, the woman, who was a little younger than Maggie's mother, had a fashionable look about her. Her square nails were painted plum and she wore a ruffled white collar.

"But of course I cannot in good conscience say the same about you—how long it's been! You've grown up entirely." She paused.

"How are your parents?" she inquired politely, glancing behind Maggie.

"My father is waiting in the car outside," she said.

"Of course." The woman trained her gaze on Maggie again. "So many people do. Especially this time of year, when it's quite lovely outside, and not too hot. Now tell me all about you." Sitting on a tall stool with hands clasped calmly before her, she seemed in no hurry to conduct official business.

"I'm here for shots," Maggie said.

The woman nodded and reached for a clipboard. "Well you never were one for chit-chat," she said without rancor, "not even as a child. So we'll get right to it. You're perhaps preparing to go into the working world?"

"I am doing that." Maggie once again felt a surge of pride in making this announcement, as well as some comfort in confirming this truth about herself. Her sleepless night had made Friday seem unreal, as though it would never arrive. "How did you know?"

"Because you asked for shots. People do that. They get immunizations, etcetera, updated, since some work places require them. And I did know you as a girl, which means that I know you're just the right age to be out on your own. All grown up and getting ready to—?" She looked to Maggie to supply the occupation.

"Take care of babies. At a daycare center in the city."

"Of course," the receptionist said, without seeming at all impressed. "Childcare only makes sense, given how much you've helped your mother over the years," she mused, "and how much you were preoccupied with playing house with my youngest son." She smiled wryly, then sighed, remembering. "Not that I blame you, as he was quite cute. And after all, if boys will be boys, then I suppose the same is true of girls. That they'll be girls, I mean."

Unsure what was meant by this, Maggie said nothing. The woman returned briskly to the main subject. "The city is, of course, well, busy and dirty, mostly, but they say that's where the young should make their start." She pulled a pen out of a jar and handed it to Maggie, then flipped the clipboard around.

Like the fat woman, the receptionist seemed to know Maggie from a time when she was younger. Maggie did not remember the son, nor any particular boy out of the town kids who had come and gone in the early years of her childhood, but lest the woman take offense, she did not confess her ignorance. Instead she looked at the paperwork and said, "I don't believe those are the kind of shots I need." She panicked, wondering if she were about to receive more shots than was strictly necessary.

"Oh?"

"No, my father thinks that I might need rabies shots." Maggie held up her bandaged finger.

"Rabies!" The woman covered her mouth with her hand. "What bit you?"

"A rat. Last night a rat bit me." She wondered whether there was any shame in having been bit by a rat. Was it her fault, or the fault of her household, somehow?

"That's terrible!" the receptionist exclaimed. A couple of women typing at desks behind her glanced up, paused a moment, then resumed their work, as if they were accustomed to the occasional empathetic display.

"I thought so," Maggie agreed, though she was somewhat alarmed by the reaction of the receptionist, especially as no one at home this morning inquired into how she had passed the night, or asked whether the bite had swelled, which it had, but only slightly.

"There's a distinct psychological horror that comes with a rat bite," the woman reflected, her expression confiding now. She leaned her elbows against the counter. "A horror that some might also attribute to receiving shots, though I would argue that they're not the same at all—the prowling and unpredictable rodent versus the antiseptic needle wielded by a friendly nurse."

"I can't remember what having a shot feels like," Maggie answered, vaguely uneasy.

"Physical pain is like that, of course—intense and apparently unendurable and then quickly forgotten. But my youngest son died when he was only thirteen and so I can attest that psychological pain, such as in grieving, can be intense and unendurable and relentless, which probably makes me more calloused toward ordinary forms of pain." She cleared her throat. "However, I retain enough perspective to be able to assure you that shots are not at all like being awakened by a wild animal in the middle of the night. So the hard part is over. In any case, I doubt the doctor will feel you need rabies shots."

"Oh?" Maggie brightened.

"There's not been a case of rabies from a rat bite here since," and here she waved her hand, "oh forever. From the beginning, really. Rats can, of course, carry rabies. In other countries, especially. But it's unusual."

"I didn't know."

"Many people don't know," the woman said. "They've no reason to know, so they never find out. Very few people are bitten by mice or rats. A bat bite, well, that's different."

"So I can go home?"

"Heavens no, I'm just the receptionist," the woman said. "Take this number and wait in one of the chairs for the nurse to call you. If the doctor chooses not to give you rabies shots, then doubtless there's some other type of vaccination you'll need, as I suspect it's been a while since you've been here." Maggie took the ticket with a red number nine on it. The receptionist patted her hand. "Don't look so worried. Perhaps you'll consider tea at my house later? For old time's sake before you depart for the city? You must have had a very difficult night."

Maggie smiled weakly and nodded, preoccupied by the dread of what was to come. Yet the suggestion of tea must have taken hold, since as she waited she began to picture large glass mugs filled with steaming black tea loaded down with heaps of cream and sugar. Strictly speaking, of course, she was not allowed to eat sugar. Still, she had consumed some the day before with the cupcake, and again during the night with the wrapper, and so was perfectly able to imagine the bitterness of the black tea leaves offset by spoonfuls of sugar. Perhaps her parents were right to be wary of sweeteners, and the visions of tea were a kind of residual opiate leftover from her previous indulgence, creating illusions that would comfort her through the deep push of the needle into the soft flesh of her body.

But by the time Maggie had been called in for her turn, then ushered out again to the lobby, she had forgotten all about the tea. She felt instead a certain measure of bravado, as if she had faced some terrible trial with dignity, even though the doctor had determined that she did not need rabies shots and the other vaccinations were mostly tolerable and over quite quickly. In her triumph, Maggie might not have remembered to wave goodbye from the front door, much less politely decline the invitation to tea, had the woman not been standing outside the entrance, waiting on her. When she spotted Maggie, she approached briskly, tiny black heels hitting the pebbles molded into the concrete.

"I've spoken with your father," she said. Over the woman's shoulder, Maggie saw her father start up the car to bring around to the front, a deceptively solicitous gesture that revealed his impatience—he had been waiting well over an hour. "You're to come to the house sometime later today to borrow my cat."

"Cat?"

"Yes. You'll need one to catch the rat. And I've got a good one. Quite the hunter and also very sweet." She patted Maggie on the shoulder and hurried on inside, just as Maggie's father gave a light tap on the car horn. "Anytime this afternoon or evening," the receptionist called over her shoulder. "I only work part-time. And we'll have that tea when you come. I do so love visits from young people, what with my own children gone."

The woman disappeared through the glass doors before Maggie could ask the way to her house. When Maggie climbed into the car, her father was out of sorts—no doubt the woman had aggravated him. He hated a busybody. In such a state, he did not mention either the woman or the cat, and so Maggie decided to wait until they reached home to ask for directions.

They weren't going home, however. "I'll drop you off in town," her father said as they pulled out of the parking lot. Doing so would save him a mile or more. This morning when his daughter awoke him, he had ascended from the depths of his unconscious through a terrible sweetness that even in his sleep he knew belonged to him only for the shortest of whiles. By the time his eyes cracked open he'd felt more loss than any experienced in waking life. Maggie thus became a witness to the last tinges of sadness which were lingering as he sat up on the couch, aching from the strange, unfamiliar bed. She was an intruder in that place, an uninvited witness, just as she was also a guide, bringing the cupcake wrapper into the house to induce such potent dreaming. He was anxious to be away from her.

"If you could leave me at the library, please," she said. She did not try to disguise her relief: she could linger at the library alone as she had not done in some time, choosing a book to keep her company these next three days, her first vacation from childcare in memory, even if she were in a sort of exile. She would savor her walk home, arriving long after the others had finished lunch, already gaining independence in her own small ways. Welcomed by both the fat lady and the receptionist, Maggie had begun to see that her house was just one place next to other places, between which she was not only able to move, but expected to do so. With practice, she would travel between places more and more easily, just as her father did, perhaps in ways that she had not yet guessed.

When they reached the square and he pulled over at the curb, Maggie stepped from the car. Before she closed the door behind her, she leaned back in. "Where do I go to get the cat?" she said.

He looked away from her and back to the road, thinking already about the solace of work, where he would be untroubled by the prospect of a cat or any other trivial concerns. "She doesn't live too far from us," he said irritably. He wished he had recalled in advance that their neighbor worked for the health department, not that it would have

done any good. "You've just got to cut through the rhododendron."
He paused, realizing that Maggie would never have gone there on
foot. Even had he not forbidden his children from trespassing on
surrounding properties, the family had lost touch with this neighbor
even before they had with Mamie. With Jocelyn, there had never been
much to lose—an awkward dinner or two before her divorce, some
small play between their young children, a neighborhood Halloween
party at Mamie's house. He had last seen Jocelyn at her son's funeral,
where at the graveside she had stared hungrily at his three sons as if
he hoarded an extra that he could do without. Then she seemed to
recall something and looked up at him just as they all did, everyone
in town staring a moment too long, as if they had discerned some
subtle disfigurement.

"You wander a little on the north side of our property and you'll
find it," he finally said, impatient with the effort and delay. "If I were
you, though," he hesitated, glancing over at her. She was leaning into
the car expectantly, dutifully ready to receive the necessary information to get the cat, maybe even to heed his warning not to go too
far or too deep into the woods. For what might she discover if she
did? "If I were you, I wouldn't roam too far." The warning was flat
and unconvincing, however, and he saw a flicker of curiosity in her
eyes, or of defiance. "After all," he put the car in gear, surprised to
find himself pleased that she would not in fact take his advice. "In
three days you'll be gone, and then you can go wherever you'd like."

CHAPTER FOUR

The elderly librarian wanted to know whether Maggie would miss her family, as they were obviously all so close. "You'll come home for visits, won't you?" she asked as she stamped the due date card.

"I don't know," Maggie said, resistant to questions demanding an appropriate response.

"What will your mother do without you?" the librarian said, her thin neck jutting from a starched blue collar. The question did not sound rhetorical, but Maggie merely smiled.

"I've enjoyed coming here," she said with less enthusiasm than she intended. She had been reading for a couple of hours in a sunny corner, and had grown sleepy and hungry. Her finger was throbbing beneath the clean bandages from the health department and her arm already felt sore from the shots.

"The library in the city is much bigger," the librarian said. "You'll like that about the place if nothing else." She hesitated, examining the book's broken spine and worn cover. "You can have this one, actually," she said, pulling the construction paper card back out of the book. She stamped "Discard" in red ink on the inside cover, then made a note of the title before returning the book to Maggie. "We'll need to replace it soon, anyway."

"Thank you," Maggie said, quite pleased, as it was a favorite.

"A parting gift," the librarian said. Then, as if she had bought permission to speak further, she clasped her bony hands together, adding, "I wonder if your mother considers your leaving evidence of a failure or a success in the grand experiment?"

"Pardon?"

"They're your mother's words, of course. Not mine. From a long time ago. I understood her to mean that she and your father were raising their children with some different ideas from their parents about how to do it."

"Oh," Maggie said, surprised by the reference to grandparents.

"It's not much different from what everyone else does, of course, but your mother had to call it something special," the librarian said. "She used to put everything in place with words—the library, an outpost of culture; your schooling, a window on the world bigger than the one the other kids looked out of; your nutrition, toxin free; your minds, as free from poison as your food." She pulled a watering can from beneath her desk. "So your leaving is evidence of something," she said, "and if you stay gone, well then that's evidence of something else."

Maggie said nothing, trying to understand whether the librarian spoke from an alliance with or hostility toward her mother. She understood only that she was being asked to evaluate a future that had not yet begun. She had never known what exactly other people pictured when they imagined the future—whether they willed their circumstances to take shape, or whether the material world gave way before them like the forest to a path, closing in behind as soon as they had passed. Finally she simply said, "I don't know about the future."

"And in that way you're no better or worse than anyone else," the librarian said, turning to fill the watering can at a sink against the wall.

Maggie fingered the torn corner of the book, thinking that she had an opportunity to ask a question that had come and gone over the years. "There's a library book I read more than once as a child," she said, "but after a long time of reading other things, I forgot the title. I wonder if you might know what it's called?"

"I might," the librarian said, turning off the faucet. "You'll have to tell me what it was about. I can't read your mind."

Maggie thought for a moment. The book had been a favorite because it was so vivid, full of texture and sound: a brown chicken egg covered with grit and mud, the ticklish asparagus frond, a swirl of muddy pond water, some cow dung buzzing with flies. Yet she had read it so long ago that now she could hardly remember what it was about, any more than she could have told her sisters a story about themselves the day before. "There was an old married couple," she began. "A farmer and his wife. Someone's grandparents, I think. They had a porch swing."

The librarian looked at Maggie strangely, but said nothing.

"I don't think much happened in the story," Maggie said, knowing that the librarian was waiting to hear the plot. She felt suddenly that she had experienced this conversation on some other occasion long ago. At the dinner table she had once asked after grandparents, a farming couple whom she'd begun to miss, and the room fell silent. Only Warren had leaned across the table to whisper, "They're from a book you read. Just some old book." She had asked the wrong question again, her parents appearing not to have heard her speak, slicing bread and spreading butter.

Now she said, "The book was really just filled with lots of descriptions of the place."

"Well it's no wonder we don't have it anymore," the librarian said, watering the primrose.

"Yes," Maggie said. "It doesn't sound very exciting." She paused. "I think I liked it because the place seemed forgotten by other people. A little neglected."

"Indeed," the librarian raised her eyebrows. "Well, I don't think I can help you without more information."

"I understand," Maggie said, disappointed. She thanked the librarian again for the book, then turned to leave. As the glass door swung shut behind her, she wondered if other young adults received more encouragement and approval for striking out than she was getting. Once on the street, Maggie knew that she couldn't count on any better reaction from the other townspeople, who did not seem to be out today as they would be tomorrow, on the family's Wednesday morning trip to the library. Passing the fire station and post office, she came to the stone apartment building where elderly women often waited outside in rocking chairs with bits of bacon tucked into biscuits for the children. Beyond the retirement home, a row of wooden houses held young mothers who often lingered outside in the warm months while their husbands performed labor elsewhere. The flower gardener gave each child a bright-colored zinnia; the music teacher sometimes let the children into her sunny front room to touch the keys of her piano, Quinn lingering tremulously over each note, reaching far with one foot to gingerly press a pedal; the sidewalk sweeper who incessantly brushed away the dust on her cracked walkway came to the fence to ask how the children were

doing in their lessons. The sweeper's own son, who had once been
Douglas' playmate from the library playground, was now always off
someplace else with his town friends.

Had any of these women been outside, Maggie might
have stopped off to politely deliver the news of her leaving,
especially since she could not trust her mother to do so tomorrow.
She did not want to disappear with so little trace that it would be
hard to find welcome should she return, something she might not
have considered before the exchange with the librarian. Yet while
passing the dark windows, she could not imagine climbing the front
porch stairs of her own initiative to ring the doorbells or knock. She
had never approached the houses of her own accord before and was
unsure of how she might be received, especially in light of the librarian's speech, which called her attention to her family's differences
with unsettling specificity. Maggie could not be sure, of course, that
there would be no spontaneous offerings of cornbread or fried pies,
no entreaties to stop in on holidays, no crocheted shawl pressed into
her hands for her first city winter. But she could not be sure that there
would be those things, either. And yet just yesterday she had entered
the fat lady's yard without any invitation at all and been served cake.

At the last house before the blacktop became gravel, a young
woman with a black braid stirred a cast iron pot suspended
from a wooden tripod. Below the tripod, a fire was burning
steadily, and a few feet away, yarn the color of goldenrod dripped
from a clothesline. On their Wednesday walks, the yarn dyer smiled
at the children, but did not cease her work, transferring the yarn
from the first pot to a second one placed on the ground, then
wrestling the heavy wet fabric onto the line. The house behind the

woman always felt vaguely familiar to Maggie, and if she stared at
the peeling blue clapboard long enough, she could sometimes picture
herself inside, hiding under a table eating a bowl of freshly whipped
cream sprinkled with sugar.

Reluctant to go home, Maggie slowed, watching the
woman that the children referred to as the witch peer down into
the caldron. Her old tee shirt was spattered with the same colors
that glinted from the fat lady's woodpile—fuchsia, turquoise, indigo.
When she straightened again, she spotted Maggie and smiled.

"I hear you'll be going away soon," she called.

Maggie stopped at the fence. "Yes," she said cautiously. She
did not expect to hear this news about herself from a near stranger.
Still, she had tired of her solitude and was now in the mood to talk,
as if her conversations with the fat lady and the receptionist and the
librarian had cultivated a new craving not unlike a craving for sweets.
"I leave in three days for the city."

"The man my mother keeps told me. He came this morning to deliver some muffins she baked." The witch briefly lifted
the golden yarn from the vat, then leaned over to check the fire.
Appearing satisfied with both, she wiped her hands on her jeans and
approached Maggie.

Maggie cringed at the thought of her name on the prowling
man's tongue, but understood that she was speaking with the fat
lady's daughter. "Your mother was very kind to me last night,"
Maggie said. She saw the witch as she had in memory the night
before, ten years younger and with her spread of black hair against
the pillow as she slept through the daylight hours, the bright red
blood of the sanitary napkin on the floor beside her. "And the cupcake

she gave me was delicious."

"Yes," the witch said briskly. "They always are. Perhaps you would like a muffin?" Without waiting for a reply, she retrieved a basket lined with a cloth napkin from the front porch.

When she returned, Maggie hesitated in a way that she had not the night before, feeling suddenly that indebtedness creates trouble, some forgotten wisdom of her father's to explain why the family did not often visit their neighbors back when such explanations were still requested. She had received a cupcake and a library book and was now taking a muffin, with a cat and a cup of tea on the horizon. What might be required in return?

She took a large bite. Blueberries were buried within the heavy dark grain.

"It's such a surprise that you really are able to leave," the witch said with a small frown, as if puzzled by a problem. She took a muffin for herself and set the basket on the ground. "So few are. My mother hasn't left. And you see that I'm still here, in spite of intentions otherwise. My father left easily enough, but he's always seemed to me to be the exception. Certainly your father couldn't bring himself to go."

Maggie was puzzled by the reference to her father's leaving, but she smiled, hoping to be agreeable. "You left the house you grew up in," she said.

"Yet I had the chance to stay away altogether," the witch said, resting one forearm against the wooden railing of the fence. "I attended craft school in the mountains. There, we learned to stain glass like my father, marbleize paper for books, hammer iron, weave baskets, throw clay. But I came home frequently for visits. My mother would bake for me, if I came home. My favorite desserts."

Maggie understood that the witch was ambivalent about her choice, and yet if she had not married, as she did not appear to have done, why not leave even now? "I'm not sure whether I'll be visiting very often," Maggie said, aware that her own future might shift and evolve in interesting ways that she could not anticipate. She had not thought of trips home at all until prompted by the librarian and now, less directly, by the witch. "Perhaps for the holidays."

The witch broke off a piece of muffin and popped it into her mouth. Chewing, she stared past Maggie as if she hadn't quite heard. "You're leaving," she finally said, "and yet I cannot help but recall just how immobilized you seemed the morning of our sleepover, when I awoke to you staring out the window, your forehead all wrinkled with worry." She trained her gaze on Maggie again, blue eyes curious.

Maggie blushed, yet she was relieved to have this memory confirmed. "I suppose I was afraid to either wake you or to leave without saying goodbye," she said. After a moment's thought, she added, "And I think I was a bit frightened of the stairs."

"As you should have been," the witched replied. "When the stairs are up, and you want to be somewhere else, you not only can't get there, you can't stop thinking about the place where you want to be—the kitchen or your father's workshop or the woods. The places don't have to be important for it to become impossible to settle back into the bedroom, even for pleasant activities. You're upstairs breathing fresh air from the open windows, but you might as well be buried."

"I can see what you mean," Maggie said with some discomfort. Indeed, the witch's description of that morning's claustrophobia caused Maggie to glimpse what it might feel like to hold one place inside of her while inhabiting another. She suddenly felt real dread of being in the church bedroom in the city, possibly torn between two places in ways that she could not now conceive. She teetered for a moment, unsure whether they had been discussing the past or the future. "I think I was also homesick," she said. She hesitated, then shyly asked, "I suppose my being silly kept us from having another sleepover?"

The witch looked at Maggie quizzically, then began to chuckle. After a moment, her laughter grew louder. A curtain fluttered at the pianist's house next door. Maggie stood rigid and bewildered, hoping for an explanation. Yet the cackling rolled on in the empty street until the young woman began to hiccup, then caught sight of the dying fire. She took a few steps across the yard before glancing back at Maggie with a smile. "Best leave while you can," the witch said, hiccupping above the smoke. "And stay safe at home until you do." She bent over to shove another log onto the fire. "People are always wanting something. Much more than they ever realize themselves. Even you."

When the woman returned to stirring her pot, Maggie felt abruptly abandoned, as if she were a failed apprentice in her trade, someone who would never learn. She thought that if the witch knew that at home she had been relegated to a hard bench at the top of the landing and to sneaking meals on the side, she might not give advice determined to box Maggie in just as soon as she had been given implicit permission by her father to roam, with the sugar she had just consumed urging her on to some new treat, perhaps tea at the receptionist's house. She turned from the fence to walk home, tired of the strong opinions and cryptic advice of strangers.

The town quickly disappeared behind Maggie, the sidewalk and blacktop rounding the bend to give way to gravel, and the stone face of the hillside rearing up to her left. On the right side of the road, a gap in the looming wall of trees offered a narrow vista of meadow sloping down to meet the forest. A large oak had fallen here in a rainstorm the previous week, shifting the view to expose a sliver of red brick and gray slate nestled amongst the canopy of trees at some distance. Silver balloons flashed in the sunlight at the edge of the brick, as if the homeowner was announcing a party. Maggie had never seen this house, which appeared to be set against the hillside to the north of their own property, beyond the rhododendron forest. With any luck, the receptionist lived there, and Maggie could avoid her own home a little longer.

The book had grown heavy in her hands, so she made a pouch for it with her cardigan, twisting the fabric like a candy wrapper and tying it around her waist so that the book lay against her lower back. Then she set off through the tall weeds. The forest below yielded the hint of an opening, a place where the underbrush had not yet been propelled forward by the surge of heat. Soon the woods would become a jungle, the poison ivy competing with the deceptively sweet honeysuckle and with the potato vine that would begin creeping along mid-summer, dangling warty beige balls like swollen ticks. Already at her feet the vines grew as if they lacked dignity or restraint, stretching, grasping, pushing pointed tips through the soil again and again, wherever there was space to fill or ground that gave before them, smothering the rusty bucket and the rose of sharon bush at the roadside. After no time at all, everything would disappear.

Maggie shuddered, stepping over a log covered with wintercreeper. She had read about the various kinds of topography and climate that swallowed its inhabitants, each in its own way—the jungles and plains and steppes, the monsoons and tidal waves and blizzards. Wading through the damp grass, she recalled an account of European explorers setting up camp in the Amazon jungle. Reptiles, insects, and vegetation swarmed their attempts at shelter, with snakes dropping on the tents like rain. The men kept fowl for food, sometimes, too, roasting rodents. One particularly vain turkey had been spoiled as the chickens and ducks were slaughtered for meals, kept beyond his time for the entertainment he provided—for his preening and for his efforts to gain alpha status through thwarted attacks on the men, who scorned him even as they let him live. On one occasion, when a beheaded duck lay thrashing on the ground, this turkey had flushed his feathers, crushed the bloody duck beneath its claws, and mounted it, imitating copulation. Maggie had put the book aside then, returning it to the library without finishing it. She understood that for the colonists far from home, this new place seemed full of the kind of morbid lust that the turkey had displayed, barren of language, a void. But even as a native, she knew that her own world was equal to those other places, making her feel as if she could barely hold onto her own bit of ground, which was always swelling with rain or drying into dust.

In the shadows at the edge of the woods, a faint path emerged as if floating on the surface of the dew-soaked grass. She took it with some relief, pulling her skirt away from the tug of beggar's lice and stepping beneath the tall poplar trees into the churned old leaves of the forest floor. After a few moments of uncertainty in which she simply dove deeper into the trees, a more distinctive path emerged, winding from her left and extending on, she hoped, in the general direction of the strange house. There had been no rain in the past few days. The ground gave beneath her boots but sprang back, without coating her in mud. As she walked, the packed dirt became increasingly shot through with roots as the poplars were replaced by the rhododendron, its thickly twined branches full of shiny leaves. Yet after ten minutes of walking, she became uneasy, the trail winding in such a way through so much of the same kind of dark crowding bush that it seemed endless and unkind. The path was well worn, and who would travel here so regularly if not tramps?

Indeed, the woods had just begun to open up again, giving her space and light, when Maggie saw two men approaching. She stopped, torn between running or hiding, when she realized that the figures were in fact her brothers, each with a loaded satchel sagging from one arm and an additional pack across the back. From behind the runner's shoulders protruded the feathery tops of carrots. They had been to market by some route unknown to her. She felt a wave of relief and also gratitude. She had never had much cause to feel thankful toward her brothers, whose workload, in comparison with her own, seemed scattered and uneven, as if infrequent weight-bearing tasks necessitated long stretches of time for recovery. Now, however, she felt a surge of appreciation.

They had not yet seen her, their eyes trained on the ground as if to view the surrounding trees would shame them, but when the runner did glance up, he came to a halt with undisguised astonishment. The theologian looked up belatedly from beneath the brown locks that hung over his eyes. He stopped a foot or two closer to Maggie, as if he were a donkey abiding by his master's signals only after delay. Without hesitation, the theologian placed his bag on the ground, eager for a break. When the runner caught up to them a moment later, however, he kept his bags on his shoulders even when he stopped in front of Maggie, resistant to any interruption. What was between the two of them, Maggie decided in this instant, was his resentment that he had not been the first born, as if taking her place in the birth order would have ensured that he would now be the one leaving the house, rather than being unable to envision himself doing so.

"I didn't know there was a short cut to the market," Maggie said, glancing beyond them. She decided not to mention the rule against trespassing that she herself would now be breaking if her father hadn't given her permission to find the receptionist's house. After all, perhaps he had been letting the boys cut across someone else's property to market for some time now. Perhaps the rules were more flexible than she had known.

"Phillip thinks it's shorter," Warren said gruffly, his shoulders slumped.

"I've timed the difference on my runs," Phillip said firmly. Beneath his blond buzz cut, beads of sweat glistened. Maggie watched as he licked one extraordinarily pink lip, uncomfortably aware of his flushed cheeks.

"I see," she said. "I hadn't known." He was waiting for an explanation for her presence here, but Maggie had none. She didn't want to mention that she was going in search of a cat.

"Are you going to the market for your own food?" Phillip asked, hoping that this was the degree to which she was being punished—perhaps she had been banned from the kitchen while he was away.

"Should I?" Maggie said. She was not sure whether to speak plaintively or in challenge, this new setting making it difficult to recall their usual forms of interaction.

Phillip hesitated. Hearing she had been bitten by a rat only slightly diminished his grudge against her for leaving him to fix dinner the previous night. He would have to discuss with his mother how they would permanently rearrange the schedule: he could picture her staring at him expectantly, waiting for him to take leadership as the more active, less bookish oldest child. But he did not want the leadership. He wanted only to nestle into various forms of comfort between the long miles. And he wanted to keep these long woodsy paths free for himself. In town, men driving by in trucks yelled "fag" at him for reasons he could not understand. He was running. He wasn't splitting wood or plowing the soil, true, but he was running, and if necessary, could keep doing so long after any pursuers gave out, wheezing on the blacktop behind him, tobacco juice dribbling from their panting mouths. Every passing season brought him no new skill and no new vision, so he did not want to meet Maggie in the woods again, some reminder of the potential of other demands on him, as if life was not in fact some soft maternal lap that he could curl up in again and again.

When Phillip did not speak, Warren shook his head, saying, "No one will be able to sleep now—not tonight, not with a rat." He nervously scratched the back of his neck.

Phillip ignored him, clearing his throat as if Maggie had laid out the terms of a deal that he must stall to negotiate. "If it's lunch you're wanting, we can save you the trip." He wanted her to be beholden to him in some way, so he pulled the carrots from the sack without taking it from his back, as if they were a sword and she the enemy he was about to face. He then reached into the bag at the theologian's feet and from the butcher's brown paper, removed a cooked sausage, a rare treat no doubt intended to console the others for her leaving.

"You'll stay gone, when you finally do go," he said, handing her the sausage, carrots, and a tomato as if they were talismans ensuring that she did not return. "Already Mother seems less—" here he hesitated, handing the theologian his bag to signal their leaving, "encumbered."

She was taken aback by this disclosure, more direct than she could recall any member of the family being with the exception of their father. In truth, Phillip looked taller, more imposing. His nostrils seemed to be flaring, as if he were running even now, the effort darkening his brow. He was angry about more than last night's meal, and the theologian, whom she always thought so abstracted with important existential questions, was carrying the burden of some practical piece of information. She glanced beyond them, wondering what lay ahead of her on the path. When she looked back at them, she saw that they were waiting, wondering if she would turn away now and return with them.

Instead of going with them, however, she tucked the carrots and tomato in her pockets, stepped around her brothers, and continued on without glancing back. She felt the boys watch her a moment, as she walked and took a bite of the delicious sausage. Then she heard the padding of the soil under their feet as they hurried along with their heavy loads. Phillip was anxious that she leave home at the same time that he was anxious that she not venture farther down the path, where he must keep some trivial secret. Still, her brothers had nothing better to barter than food. They had nothing else that she needed, not their bare rooms or dusty books or private lusts. Let them have the house, let it hold them.

CHAPTER FIVE

As the woods gave way to a clearing, Maggie saw that the silver balloons were somehow tethered to the front of a two-story brick home, which perched on a hill covered with hemlocks. The house had something of a grand appearance, with a steeply peaked roof, a wrap-around porch, and a long staircase leading up the grassy slope. After a moment, the front door opened and a woman came out onto the porch, waving. Surely this was the receptionist? Maggie waved back uncertainly.

Crossing the meadow to the base of the hill, Maggie quickly finished the sausage and crammed the carrots and tomato deeper into her pockets. When she came closer, she indeed recognized the receptionist smiling at her from the top of the staircase.

Maggie had found the house without any remarkable effort, yet the climb up the flight of stairs made her unaccountably tired, as if the rest of life were to be some version of climbing up things in order only to climb back down again, having gained very little. The hemlock trees were shedding, forcing her to wade through the dead brown needles that stuck to her tights above her low boots. She paused to shake off the needles. She should have been employing herself in other ways—cutting a pattern for a third dress, reading a book about the city from the library—instead of borrowing a cat to safeguard a household she was intending to leave. Still, she would most certainly sleep better tonight without fear of rats.

"How lovely to see you, dear!" the receptionist called, startling Maggie with a hug as soon as she reached the top of the stairs. Maggie thought that, aside from the director at the church, the receptionist was the most fashionable woman she had ever seen. She had changed from her skirt and jacket into jeans and a soft gold sweater. Without her makeup, she looked younger, her tousled gold hair framing ruddy checks. Behind her, the balloons floated high above the open porch, their red ribbons tucked beneath a plant pot on the brick ledge.

"You're earlier than I expected—such a nice surprise."

"I saw your balloons from the road," Maggie said.

"Aren't they lovely?" the receptionist said. She crossed the porch and lifted the pot to retrieve the handful of ribbons. "I do so like an extra bit of shine. And then they bring in the guests like crows." She gestured for Maggie to precede her into the house. "Please come in," she said. "I'm home from work just a little while ago. You've missed my mid-afternoon snack, but I'll make us some tea."

Maggie entered a spacious foyer with a staircase at the back and large empty rooms with shining wood floors on each side. The woman released the balloons to float toward the ceiling and led Maggie through a door near the base of the stairs.

"Did you move here recently?" Maggie asked, following the receptionist into the kitchen. The receptionist laughed, motioning for her to sit at a small table with two wooden chairs. "I can see why you'd think that," she said, picking up some empty cupcake wrappers from the table and tossing them into the trashcan. Maggie recognized them as the fat lady's pink wrappers, and wished she could retrieve them from the garbage to suck on the pulp soaked in sugar. "My things are upstairs," her hostess continued, wiping the tabletop with a dishrag. "My ex-husband was a military man. An important one. I can't think what all that means except that he was powerful and decisive, and when he left a few years ago he took most of the furniture." She shrugged, turning to the stove to retrieve the silver kettle, which she held under the tap. "The furniture wasn't very pretty, actually," she said. "And there was so little of it, as we'd moved around so much already." She set the kettle on the stove and leaned against the counter to wait for the water to boil. "I think now that it was really rather unnecessary all along. Furniture lets you sit in different places and at different angles, presumably for different purposes, but I find that one good chair in the right spot outweighs a large number of them in various locations." She smiled. "In any case, if you're to become a regular guest, you'll have to have a look around, see if you can find a good place for a chair."

Maggie did not remind the woman that she was leaving soon for the city. Instead she said, "Those look familiar," and pointed to the mugs she had envisioned while waiting at the health department that morning.

"Ah yes. Only because you loved my tea so much, I suspect. You wanted the glass mugs so you could make sure the tea was just the right color. I quite overload it with sugar and milk. Your parents were horrified, as at home you drank only plain herbal teas. Drink, I suppose. But they were too polite to protest much. Most children who are not fed sugar at home never want it at all. It's a bit of an acquired taste. An addiction, some might argue. But you had a natural sweet tooth." She dumped three heaping teaspoons of sugar in each mug, then poured in the cream from the refrigerator. "In any case, it's hardly tea anymore, when I'm finished with it, and so it will make up for my having eaten the last of the cupcakes before your arrival. How is the rat bite, by the way? How are the shot sites?"

Maggie looked at the bandage, which had accumulated sweat and dust. "I don't really know," she said.

"Well, that won't do," chided the receptionist, catching the kettle before it reached full pitch and pouring the water over the teabags. "You'll get an infection, if you neglect it. You'll want to redress it when you get home. I'd do it now, but you'll be handling a cat before all is said and done. Best to do it afterward."

Maggie warmed with this attention, wondering with belated sorrow whether Phillip was right that their mother felt burdened by her presence. Here with the receptionist, Maggie felt wanted, as if she were helping to enrich her neighbor's afternoon just by quietly consuming a hot beverage. She also felt that her company was preferred in a way that it had not been at the fat lady's house, who had listened to her talk of the city willingly enough, but fed everyone without apparent discrimination. While they drank their tea, the receptionist chatted cheerfully about the health problems she witnessed at work, warning Maggie about the kinds of illness she might catch from the children she'd be caring for, after being so long cloistered in her own home. Maggie was content to let her talk, finding herself worn out by the day's unusual social exertions. The practical references to her future life away from home were reassuring: the many conversations she'd had that morning had given her the unsettling feeling that no one actually expected her to go.

"Though of course you'll not be in the city for long," the receptionist said. "There are so many other places in the world to make a
living that there's no use getting attached to one idea." She spoke as
if envisioning bigger, more glamorous cities elsewhere where Maggie
might attend to captivating children in wealthy households, destined
by her native talents to escape ordinary work. As the receptionist
talked on about her travels with her husband, Maggie imagined such
success for herself, fueled not only by the receptionist's language,
which washed over Maggie in luxurious excess, but by stories she had
read—stories where people unencumbered by babies took unusual
forms of transportation through striking landscapes, all the while
chatting comfortably with interesting strangers. She would be flushed
with the pursuit of texture and scent and sound, collecting sensations
that she would not crate or contain but simply lie down in, speaking
some other language she had not yet learned.

Distracted by these daydreams, Maggie gazed out the windows
above the sink. Behind the house, a paved driveway too steep to
use led to a garage where a long blue sedan was parked. Maggie
pictured leaning back against the concrete crest of the hill in this
sunny spot, lying there until wet from sweat. The boy's hand she was
holding in memory became slippery, and beneath them, the plastic
sled felt sticky. They were pretending they were about to slide from
the driveway right down into the basement, in homage to a rhyme
they often chanted together—*slide down my rain barrel, into my cellar
door, and we'll be jolly friends, forever more.* If they believed strongly
enough, the driveway would become a waterslide, sending them
through the basement and out the other side of the house, where it
would twist to connect with the brick gutter beneath the hemlock

trees, a chute covered with so many needles that you could slide all the way to the runoff pipe at the bottom and farther, to the large culvert where the tramps sheltered from the rain and cold. Or so she had told her playmate, as they lay against the driveway, but he had already moved to the next verse of the song: *Oh Ceci enemy, come out and fight with me, and bring your soldiers three. Climb up my thorny tree. Slide down my razor blade, into some alcohol, and we'll be jolly enemies, forever more, more, more.*

She reached down to tug sleepily at her tights, trying to recall the rest of the lyrics, and in doing so, realized that the receptionist had stopped speaking. Maggie had been cloaked warmly in speech, comfortably half-listening to anecdotes. Now her neighbor was standing to collect their mugs, leaving the kitchen cool and dusky. "Thank you for the tea," Maggie said reflexively, unsure of when, precisely, she had stopped listening, or whether she had neglected some more considerate response.

"You're quite welcome," the receptionist replied, but in rinsing the dishes she had her back to Maggie, and for a fleeting moment Maggie felt the hard and lonely place that was locked into the empty house. She shivered. "You're absolutely right, my dear," the receptionist said, turning toward her, the shadows gathered in the permanent furrows of her brow, so that she appeared to be frowning. "It's grown chilly while we've talked—the steam never kicks on in spring." Her voice seemed to join with the rhyme still echoing in Maggie's mind. "I suspect I've made you miss your supper—though it looks as if you're carrying yours with you." She glanced at the carrot fronds emerging from Maggie's dress pocket with a small smile.

"A snack," Maggie said, looking down at herself. Droplets of blood from the night before stained her skirt. "I had forgotten."

"I had thought that Lula might make an appearance," the receptionist said, bending to rub the dishcloth over a drizzle of dried pink icing she had missed before, "but she's being shy. Or rather lazy." She tossed the rag into the sink, but Maggie continued to stare at the spot where the icing had been, seeing instead her brother Phillip's thin pink lip. "I'll go upstairs and get her."

Maggie followed the receptionist through the kitchen to the hall. Surely the pink of Phillip's lip had been unnatural, his apparent need for her to not discover something beyond the edge of the woods some indication that he had a secret to keep to himself. If so, then Maggie had been feeling more special than was strictly appropriate, without even a cupcake saved for her visit. Yet surely her hostess would have mentioned her brothers dropping by. Her brothers might want to keep this secret to themselves, hoarding the sweet tea and the attention and the long spells of language that would both intoxicate and shame them, but the receptionist would have no reason not to disclose a visit had they made one.

Ahead of her, the receptionist turned at the base of the stairs. "You're welcome to simply stay here overnight, of course," she said, "to avoid another sleepless night with a rat afoot. The extra bed is always made up."

Maggie hesitated at the offer. "You're very kind," she faltered, "but I suppose my family would worry." She was not at all convinced that her family would worry, but she wanted the receptionist to do so—worry about her walk home through the woods among tramps, about getting a good warm meal, about being protected from the other children—yet of course Maggie was too old for that, and there were no other children now.

"Well I would phone them, of course," the receptionist said, "but I suspect it would feel strange to sleep away from home after all these years. Plenty of that ahead of you in the city." She turned to climb the stairs, calling to the cat. Maggie realized with some disappointment that she had hoped the receptionist would ask again, would insist, would for a moment rob Maggie of the exertion of will that she saw was to be the central component of adult life.

In the hall where Maggie stood waiting, the sun shone through the front glass and rested on the framed picture of a young boy hanging from the wall. He was blond and wearing a baseball shirt smeared with red clay. Maggie stared at him absent-mindedly, this older version of her childhood playmate foreign to her. She listened as the woman called the cat, her tone changing from searching to soothing, the whispers echoing in the bare stairwell until the sounds contorted and Maggie thought she also heard her own mother speaking in a harsh tone of recrimination, a warning, as if an exchange were taking place on the landing. Yet when the woman appeared, she was alone and carrying a huge long-haired cat with a smashed face. She cradled it over one shoulder, the cat's fur dark black with a section of lighter brown around its middle, as if it were a wooly worm caterpillar, predicting the winter weather.

"You recognize my son, I see," the woman said sadly, glancing at the photograph.

"He was your youngest," Maggie said, and felt buoyed suddenly, with the ground wavering unsteadily beneath her, as if she had been thrown into the air and over a shoulder, with the slippery hemlock needles beneath someone else's sure feet. Though there was only his bone and muscle beneath her hip, she could feel within the boy the strong force of love that he had for his father. She remembered, too, the accompanying hatred of his own weakness and failure, as if the tiny flaw that had caused his heart to suddenly give out was already known to him, a secret shame he hoped to be able to disguise with bright smiles. "But," Maggie said, "he died." She immediately regretted speaking so bluntly.

The receptionist, however, didn't seem to mind. "He was too good for this world," she said, staring at the photo with apparent indifference. "And yet," she continued, "he is the only one of the two to remain, in a manner of speaking. His other brother, who knows?" She shrugged to indicate that she did not know where he was and perhaps did not care, hoisting and re-nestling the cat in the process. Yet Maggie could feel the two absent sons spiraling within the woman, who wanted her universe to stop spinning as it never would, in the same way that, back home, her own mother wanted to bring Bertie back to her breast. "You'll forgive me when I say that children are capable of such ungracious forms of neglect."

"As are husbands," Maggie said, taking her cue from the fat lady. Then, without thinking, she added, "But not mothers?"

The receptionist grew rigid, one eyebrow arched. "Everyone wants a mother," she said. "And so mothers are always to be blamed. But never forgotten. Haunting is our one form of recompense for intolerable heartbreak and suffering." She smiled politely as if Maggie had said something discourteous about an exquisite pastry she had been served in good faith, then held out the cat. "Adult children are almost impossible to love. My youngest son died at a good time, really."

Maggie barely heard this last declaration in her attempts to find the right way to grasp the cat, which was dangling languidly in mid-air. Having never had a cat of her own, she was unsure of how to hold this one, but found her so compliant that she simply placed her over one shoulder as if she were burping her youngest brother again. She felt the fur against her neck and the purring vibration against her heart and the tiny bones beneath her fingertips. The cat's head dropped over her shoulder like a dish towel. Already she could feel her growing heavy in her arms, and wished for a carrying case.

"She's beautiful," Maggie said, wondering what was being asked for in exchange. "Where did you get her?"

The receptionist walked toward the front door. "She was dropped in the neighborhood. Can you imagine that? A full-blooded Persian. And pregnant when dropped." She laughed strangely. "She's perhaps too well bred. A terrible mother. When she gave birth she dragged her newborn kittens around the kitchen by the umbilical cord. I had to cut them lose myself with scissors. And before I even realized she was in labor, she had already half-eaten the first herself." She wrinkled her nose and sighed. Maggie felt the weight of the cat against her anew, as if she carried an ominous indifferent force. "They all died, of course, as anyone might without a mother's love. I couldn't bottle feed them enough—couldn't keep them warm enough—couldn't take them to work." She stared sadly at the cat for a moment, then opened the door for Maggie. "Well, enough of that. We'll make arrangements for her return sometime soon." She patted Maggie's arm. "I've so enjoyed your visit."

Maggie assured her neighbor that she would take good care of her cat and said goodbye. When the door closed behind her, she briefly hesitated at the view. From here, she could look back down the hill and see the woods broken apart with fields, and to the far left, the tin roof of her own house barely breaking through the crown of the trees. She did not linger, however, and at the bottom of the stairs, she picked up speed and walked quickly across the field, the book she had tied back around her waist now as heavy as the cat. Maggie was glad to have the house recede behind her, feeling as though she had missed some significance to her interaction with the receptionist, some layer of meaning that would make itself evident at an inopportune time. And yet when her mind tried to settle on what those moments and meanings might be, she felt them escape in the surge of caffeine and sugar from the tea that caused her heartbeat to ripple and dip.

Maggie could only just see her way through the dim woods, where she intended to return in the direction that the boys had taken, bypassing the road. As she slowed to wind through the rhododendron, she felt the cat begin to purr again. Together they were twisting their way along the path when for a moment Maggie had the sense that, like the cat, she was also being carried, suspended, bounced about as a wheelbarrow beneath her bumped across a root. She gripped the sides of the rusting metal, unable to balance with any other part of her body since her legs were bound by a tube of green fabric with shiny blue thread that began across her chest and ended beyond her toes in the shape of a mermaid's tail. The tail stuffed with fin-shaped cardboard fanned over the end of the wheelbarrow, hiding her tennis shoes, though she would do no walking, only hopping, when they arrived at the fat lady's house for orange cupcakes with black plastic spiders on top. She was a mermaid on dry land, unable to maneuver, dependent on others, a long way from home. But when she had looked back to urge the bearer of the burden faster along the path, she could only see a blur of pale skin, a shock of light hair, a fading presence that said he would fail her, if not at this task, then others. Behind him, the tall shadow of his older brother loomed, as if death kept coming even for those already turned ghost.

When Maggie finally emerged into the clearing of her own backyard she stopped, arms shaking. She sat down in the grass to rest, repositioning Lula in the well that her skirt made when she crossed her legs. Hearing through the open windows the ringing of pots against the porcelain sink, she decided that it was too early yet to enter the house. Her own need for food pronounced, she took from her pockets the tomato and the bunch of carrots, both of which the Persian sniffed before losing interest. Maggie hoped her mother had been saving the chicken livers, freezing them to cook with onions and gravy, so she could feed some to the cat. She took a bite of carrot, noting the strange contrast between the contented vibration of the cat's purr and the killing and eating of which she was capable. Lula would have reabsorbed the nutrients from her kitten, digesting the small parts her body had created, recycling each cell and molecule all at once, rather than feeding on her offspring over and over again during the course of their lives. Or was it the other way around, with the children feeding on the mother? Maggie had the feeling that she was holding in her arms her imaginary grandmother, the one who had killed some of her own babies with a coat hanger and then laughed about it afterwards.

In the house, a light came on behind the thin curtain concealing the theologian's room, through which no one would think to peer at his bent and flaccid form over the great texts. Another illuminated the landing, where after a moment's interlude, Maggie could see the silhouette of her father approach the window, his round chin lifted toward some point far off on the horizon, shoulders settled and soft in a rare moment of abandon. To the right of the landing, the light in her old room came on, and she saw Douglas sitting on the bed with his knees crossed, reading a book and perhaps waiting for her father to move again, holding his breath in that way that he would—that to some degree they all would, as with a stranger in the house—until their father passed by.

For the first time in years, Maggie sat in the meadow staring back at the house that in dusk had become like a doll's, showing its inner workings as the sun reflected against the peeling white clapboard. A great deal of space extended from her tiny bedroom to the southern end of the house, which she had always pictured hovering just beyond her closet and her parents' half bath. In this long stretch of outside wall, a round window was suspended, presumably the window to the bathroom, a room she had seen even less of than her parents' bedroom. Yet she did not recall the bathroom having a window.

Her father turned from gazing across the fields, but did not turn out the light when he passed her bench and entered the nursery. He was only going to retrieve a book for reading in the living room, then, since none of them left lights on unnecessarily. In her parents' room, gray dusk would be gathering amongst the furniture and the folds of the bedspread. Would the bathroom door be opened or closed? She waited, imagining her father moving about in the shadows, reaching for the book on his bureau or among discarded clothes on a cane-bottom chair. Still, the small round window remained dark. She stared at it while the color drained from the world around her, long after her father again appeared on the landing and then descended the stairs, leaving behind him some small space she had not accounted for, with cracks through which a blast of cold air had just whistled.

CHAPTER SIX

The morning after her eldest brought home the neighbor's cat, Hannah awoke early, nightgown bunched uncomfortably around her knees beneath the blanket, bare feet cold in the chill. With Martin sleeping beside her as usual, rather than on the couch downstairs, she was also her usual self, watchful before the start of day.

She had slept so well the night before, and rose with such liberation in the morning, filled with an ease of spirit that helped relieve the ache of Maggie's leaving. For years she had been able to wake in an instant when one of her children needed her, then quickly return to deepest sleep once the problem was solved. But a new form of sleep had emerged sometime after Edwin was born, a twilight state that blurred the boundaries between waking and sleeping, day and night. She'd been unable to detect her urgent need to no longer share a bed with her husband, who filled the room with his presence, never a man to be ignored.

With the night mind's gravitation toward possible truths and grand solutions, she considered unlikely new arrangements that would give her a room, as if material existence would alter for her desires: the basement, unfinished and now, evidently, occupied by rats; an old storm cellar, built by the owners of the original house that had burned down long ago, to be replaced by this odd collection of small and large rooms, an eccentric design that had made the house more affordable; a tool shed where they kept piles of wood and where her husband sometimes went to smoke; a barn with full inches between worn wooden slats and a growing tilt to the entire structure, as if Edwin's bouncing ball had slowly caused it to lean; and finally, someplace else that she seemed to have forgotten, slipping just out of reach, elusive and undefined. She felt a growing unease. She had never before come to terms with the limitations imposed by the architecture of the house. Yet she had to have her own room if nothing else.

Thus she began, as she had not done for years now—how many years?—to consider her children's futures—futures that might surrender a bedroom to her. Phillip was most likely to leave next, using the same skills that caused her to depend upon him: some comfort with the world, some ability to negotiate the challenges that had gradually proved too much for her. She had wanted to build a refuge for all of them and could not remember the point at which she had begun to turn away so often that she struggled to turn back, just as she had with her husband and he with her, the two of them always lying back to back. Still, she might be able to tolerate engaging with the world again if she could only experience nightly renewal, each day's small death leading to morning rebirth—surely this was how other people managed. Phillip had given no sign that he would leave beyond his long runs in the countryside, yet when he arrived home from the market yesterday and set the bags on the dining room table, he was newly alert to something, and his brother, in his own drooping, lethargic way, was also alert to this thing, which he pushed away by returning to his room and leaving his brother to put away the groceries. And why hadn't Phillip complained of this negligence? She had looked away from them, from whatever tension they shared, back to Bertie's drawing.

Hannah carefully sat up in bed, reached for the water glass from the nightstand, and took a sip. Certainly Warren would not go anywhere anytime soon, or would break her heart in the going, so sure was she that her eldest son would be unable to sustain the vision of the world that he had cultivated within the walls of his room, and would be unable to survive the loss of that vision, accommodating all of those contradictory pieces. In an argument long ago, her husband had complained bitterly that this son in particular needed a "dose of reality," as if the reality that Warren experienced right here at home was somehow illusory, inadequate, not fully formed, while authentic realities were out there for those brave enough to confront them. As if knowledge of business or crime or drugs or women was the last frontier in knowing, the ground of existence, the way things really were at their most real that everyone needed to know about. No, one hardly needed to leave the house to experience the harrowing range of emotional possibilities in this world—neglect and doubt, deception and rage. Her son could continue to build his system of ideas for as long as they could support him. He would sustain others in their more tawdry pursuits by his meditative devotion to a series of truths—sustain Maggie even, traipsing around the countryside for the last day as if she were truly free, as if such freedom were possible. Hannah suspected that the world that her son inhabited still had its pockets of darkness, and that if he worked long enough he could fill those pockets with light, generating hope for her like a living furnace below her bedroom—what was now her bedroom.

She was unsure about her two oldest boys, but Douglas would have to go. Would have to be convinced, could in fact be easily convinced to follow in his father's footsteps to the city, leaving her with his room. He was already restless, and unlike the other boys, he adored his father, for all the good it did him. He would need two years to grow and to cultivate a skill. She would need him to do less school work, which lately made him petulant anyway, and more yard work and landscaping, both here and at the houses in town, to give him the start in the working world that Maggie had. If any of them decided to pursue further education, they would have to find their own way. Her children would have this sanctuary within the wilderness long after the other illusions dropped away, as hers had done, so that she no longer believed books alone could transform lives that ultimately consisted of the same grinding components—economics, relationships, and the burden of consciousness that knowledge did not lift.

When the light finally broke in the room, Hannah had made a decision for the first time in years. In a couple of weeks, their schooling would break for the summer anyway, and so today she would ask Douglas to trim the hedges. She would ask him to mow. She would let him do so in lieu of lessons, which was the only way that he would not feel put upon, not just today, but in the days to come as she gave him additional chores and some small challenges—a new frame for the neglected vegetable garden, a trip to the hardware store for pine straw to spread beneath the azalea bushes that were choked by weeds, a repair to the retaining wall in the front yard—tasks that would generate enough ownership and pride that he would not complain. She would look for books on the subject today. She would begin—and here she took a deep breath—she could surely begin to talk to the town folk about having a young man who was willing to mow. She would have to, with Maggie gone.

"Martin?" she said.

Her husband didn't respond, but he was listening. He had come awake in the last few minutes, snores ceasing as dawn filtered into the room.

"Douglas will clip the hedges today. And do some mowing. You'll want to ask him to do so yourself. And when you get home from work, if you could compliment him."

"Oh?" he said, sounding only mildly interested.

"One compliment," she said. "That's all that's required."

"It's Wednesday," he said. "It will be dark when I get home."

She felt a familiar mix of relief and anxiety at being reminded of the day. "In the morning then." She rose and pushed back the curtain. Over the valley hung a dim mist. From somewhere in the house came the mewing of the cat. The front door closed. Maggie was up.

On his side of the bed, Martin sat up and stretched, hearing the cat and once again feeling disgust at that woman Jocelyn's officious offer of her pet the day before, giving them another mouth to feed. He had been surprised at how quickly he had agreed to it, truly frightened that another of his children would be bitten. "No rat traps, now," Jocelyn had warned him, long nails clicking at the side of his station wagon. "Not with Lula roaming around your property." And he had agreed, because no matter what his old neighbors thought—that he was rude, aloof, distanced for reasons they all flattered themselves they understood—he still did not want to harm a cat or see his children bitten by rats. Otherwise, he would have declined the offer, safely refusing any indebtedness. Jocelyn reminded him of his own mother, her gifts and sacrifices accompanied by expectations that were no less forceful for being elusive. Even though his mother had cut off all contact with him nearly a decade ago, he could still feel her needing something from him, as if her silence were some kind of obstacle he was failing to overcome. Still, Maggie would be gone shortly, and there would be no call for any of them to see the neighbor again beyond returning the cat, who Jocelyn had assured him wouldn't wander far afield.

Having dressed and used the restroom, he quietly slipped out the bedroom door, so as not to wake the children. He felt as he always did when he crossed his children's room: that he had interrupted some quiet drama, some subversive communication that halted upon his entry and resumed upon his exit, as if their silence was an ironic subterfuge intended to mock him. Yet they were all only sleeping, the littlest barely stirring in his new bunk bed as if the consciousness of his mother was calling to him to prepare for their morning reunion.

Before he descended the stairs, Martin saw that Douglas was already up and out, then caught a glimpse of Maggie from the western window of the landing, with the Persian lolling nearby and Phillip jogging from the yard in the direction of the rhododendron forest. Maggie knelt on an old blanket in the grass, her sleeves rolled to her elbows, washing yesterday's denim dress in a wide bucket, rinsing in another. He felt a pang of pity—she was up early, probably having slept badly. She was staying out of the bathroom to allow the family to complete its morning routine and was choosing not to run the washing machine without a full load, since the rest of them had done laundry the day before. Still, as with other people, so much of her suffering was of her own making. If she should overcome her aversion to the couch, she could sleep there instead of the bench. She should have washed in the tub the evening before, especially since the dress and the sheet would already be bloodstained from the delay. In yesterday's visit to the health department and to Jocelyn's, she had been so like her mother, negligent and careless about her appearance, bloodied and unaware of the kind of impression she might be making, instead of choosing the clean gray dress with pink roses that she now wore. Now she scrubbed like a washerwoman in the yard, her forearms red and shining as his own mother's had been when he was a child, before indoor plumbing, before her long-winded confidences had pushed him into his own solitary space, where language did not enter to confuse and manipulate. He felt a surge of hope that Maggie would make it away from this place, not only in the city but somewhere else, in other cities or other regions, in a way that he had not. As for the others, they were products of this place—let them stay here, ministering to him in his old age.

Behind Martin, the children's bedroom door opened and their mother appeared, Bertie on her hip, his long legs dangling. She stopped, startled at the sight of her husband still on the landing.

"Where's Maggie?" she said, just for something to say. She saw the book jutting out from beneath the pillow and wondered how it was that these tales she had taught her children to value would assist her eldest come Friday. Lately they all came up from reading as if at the end of a morphine drip, incapable of making the transition into the concrete reality of their surroundings, anxious to plunge back down again. When Hannah had read as a child, her mother would stare at her through a cloud of cigarette smoke and say, "You're so smart.

You must know a lot from all that reading." Hannah knew this was not what was happening as she read—she was not getting smarter by reading stories. She also understood that she was not receiving a compliment, especially when it was followed by the question, "Do you have a boyfriend? Do you have a little boyfriend yet?" Boys was the subject at which her mother could excel—how duplicitous they were, how fleeting in their affections. She discussed the subject prematurely, when she could still be an authority on heartbreak and lies before her daughter left to box herself in with the kind of man who could not be trusted.

Which she had of course done, in ways that were not quite clear, her husband now looking away from her without speaking.

Martin listened to the comforting footfalls of the awakened children as he descended the stairs. Nearly everything in this place fit and formed around him, trapping him, suspending him, supporting him. Nearly everything was, in some way, about him. Even on those days that he came home and feared for a moment that the members of his family did not need him, he would sense the patterns they held shift and alter in his presence, in many cases for the good—fights forgotten, ambling thoughts focused again, sense of purpose renewed—and he was reassured. Unlike the men he met in the city, who tonight over drinks would grumble about wanting freedom from the facade of family and from the prejudices of culture and religion, he had never been able to weigh his desires in favor of leaving. Both he and his wife had been only children, their childhood longing for siblings transforming into a yearning for a large family that would strengthen their attachment to this place where they were raised. He had never wanted to jog away as his son had just done—his son with some

small secret. For Phillip had a look of late, greedy and full, starved
and bursting, the appetites vying against one another.

* * * *

Maggie knelt beside the wash pan in the backyard, glancing up
as her father let the screen door fall behind him. He gave a gruff
good morning, a rare greeting indicating that he had seen the
bloody rat curled on their back doorstep, where Lula had dragged
it from the kitchen like an obedient dog. He stooped to collect the
dead animal with his work gloves as Maggie had chosen not to do,
wanting him to know the cat's worth. She kept her elbows deep
in the sudsy water, bent on ignoring whatever criticism her father
might be making.

But he walked on without further comment, heading toward
the shed, where a shadow passed across the window. Maggie saw
that Douglas was once again perched inside on the work bench, as
if spinning gold from scraps of metal and garden tools. He was
brooding in his solitude, a deck of cards or his father's pipe for
company, unhappy that today he would have to go with the younger
children to the playground and then the library. He had lately been
dragging on these walks, sullen in their stops at neighbors' front yards,
uncomfortable with his in-between status while his older brothers
enjoyed independence. Still, this isolation would not suit him, either,
she was certain. Sleeping alone. Playing alone. As the firstborn, she
had not needed an ally, but Douglas appeared awash in the middle,
searching the shore after some long-forgotten shipwreck. Maggie
remembered a time long ago when she had watched Douglas await a

visit from his friend in town. She had been holding the baby Edwin in the nursery, showing him things from the window that he seemed indifferent to as people do with babies—his reflection in the glass, the first red leaf of fall on the sugar maple in the front yard. Below, Douglas stood on the front walkway with a red scarf, eager to build a fort in the cedar forest to the south of the house, all of the long- ing that he possessed directed at this project and at the boy whose friendship the project depended upon. He chattered long about their progress when she tucked him in each night.

Maggie did not remember when that boy had stopped coming— when he had chosen to play with the boys in town instead, always either at school or "off someplace," his mother said when they passed by on their trips to the library.

This morning, pouring the gray water from the buckets, knowing her finger would have to be bandaged yet again, Maggie resisted the temptation to look up at the house, to examine the knots and joints and seams, the peeling paint and crooked gutters, and most of all the single round window. As soon as she had come outside she felt a disorienting tilt, as if the house had spilt her onto the grass like tea from a teacup, no longer trusting her with its secrets. The night before, she had gone to bed full, anxious that the smell of cheese lingered from her solitary reheating of the leftover squash casserole. With Lula purring beside her on the bench, she mentally mapped the closets and cupboards, entrances and exits, the dips in the worn wooden stairs and the chips in the molding, searching for the gaps in her memory. She moved toward each family member's sleeping consciousness as if there, too, she might find some access to hidden interiors. But the household remained fortified against her, the wall clock in the dining room ticking, the crickets sounding timid beyond the open windows.

Now she wrung more water from the wet things to avoid her father, who was walking toward his car with a bag of cold breakfast, eager to arrive at work early today. When he had safely driven away, she gathered the laundry in the blanket she had been kneeling on and crossed the yard. At the clothesline, she took wooden pins from her pockets and hung the linens, her dress and underwear, and the pair of tights that it was warm enough today to do without. After a moment in which she was waiting only to fool herself, feigning indifference for the sake of an invisible audience, she turned to examine the southern end of the house. On the second floor she saw the square window she had remembered in her parents' room that would be centered over their bed. From each side of this window stretched the exterior of the house with only one additional window to the left for the half bath. Otherwise, blank space extended above the windows of the first floor—one in Warren's room and two large ones marking the dining room. Within that blank space would be the bed, bureaus, a sewing table, and a chair to rock a baby to sleep. Nothing more. Yet she found herself staring at the far left corner, wringing the fabric yet again, waiting for the rest of the family to appear for their morning excursion.

In a moment, the back door opened and the children came around the house carrying buttered biscuits, their once-a-week break from a formal hot breakfast. Behind them, their mother seemed unusually purposeful in her stride, with a bag full of books and Bertie by her side. They were setting out to prove to Maggie that they could accomplish a trip to the library without her, Ellen the only one to smile and raise a hand in departure. As the children disappeared behind the front of the house, Maggie realized Douglas had not been among them. Instead, the noise of the lawn mower in the back meadow startled Lula from where she had been lounging in front of the cellar door. Douglas, apparently exempt from library day, was now mowing afresh last year's paths.

The house was empty—nearly empty, with Warren in his room. Maggie was leaving soon, perhaps not to return. She had never been in the house alone—had never had a day at home when all of the others were away, never faked an illness on library day to stay curled up in bed. She had no idea what Warren did in their absence, though she had often envied his solitude. She always pictured him only continuing to read, but yesterday, seeing that he and Phillip might have a secret, she wondered if there was something else for Warren, something small and simple like a long bath, after which he would linger before the mirror to examine his features, whistling to himself. And in thinking of what it was that he did in the empty house, she decided that today she would fail them all—fail to help carry the books to the library, fail to leave Warren alone with his philosophical musings, and fail to follow the unspoken rule against entering their parents' room without permission. Instead, she would pry.

When Maggie opened the screen door, Lula appeared beside her and slid through, taking a new position beside the open basement door where she began licking herself. Maggie ignored her, passing into the dining room where the wood stove and chairs and table all sat in attendance, waiting on the human drama to reanimate them. Then she climbed the stairs.

On the landing she wandered into the children's room, which felt warm and comfortable, perhaps the most welcoming room in the house, without any uneasy associations except for their parents' door, shut as always on the far wall. Being in her old room alone summoned an elemental longing—product of the secrecy and trespassing of this moment, small transgressions that reminded her of when she was little and first discovered the pleasure of sneaking upstairs to wedge a rag doll between her thighs. She squelched the impulse to indulge the feeling now, but when she crossed the room to open her parents' door, the desire disappeared altogether on its own.

Light from the square southern window illuminated a room shaped and arranged much as Maggie remembered it. A cream quilt lay smoothly over the bed, with a nightstand on the left side and a cane-bottom chair on the right next to the closed bathroom door. Bright rag rugs had been placed on each side of the bed, the only real color in the room. A chest of drawers was positioned next to her parents' long closet on the inside wall. On top of the bureau an empty letter holder made of swirling brown glass glinted, its beauty surprising Maggie in the otherwise plain room. Her father had taken an unusual liking to the object at an outdoor craft market in town many years ago, also buying her a head wreath made of paper flowers, a rare treat that now dangled from Agnes' bedpost, faded and worn. Otherwise, the room was bare of artifacts or curios, jewelry or flowers, baskets or boxes. A window from the front side of the house lit her mother's sewing corner, with a table for cutting patterns, a rocking chair for handwork, and the machine itself, requiring a skill that Maggie had not mastered, since it was only pulled into the living room a couple of times a year.

Maggie had not seen this room in years and yet there was nothing to see. She felt vaguely disappointed, a rare but not entirely unfamiliar feeling that now conjured up a fragment of memory in which she leaned over a large trunk in some strange house long ago, expecting to discover the treasures that the books had always promised—bits of costume jewelry, a compass, a dented metal flute, a frayed bonnet or suede gloves—but finding only the most ordinary and useful of items, telling their predictable stories: someone's old baby clothes, a few monogrammed towels. She wanted to stock her own trunk with antiques, then cast a spell of forgetting, rediscovering it later all in a jumble. But when she tried now to remember where the dull trunk had been, she could not be sure that she hadn't simply read about it.

Maggie stared at the bathroom door for one long moment, then turned to cross the room in the opposite direction. Inside her parents' closet hung a row of her father's suits, a pair of overalls, and some flannel shirts. On her mother's side were a few everyday dresses, a long black winter coat, and a brown rain coat with a belt, all familiar items. Old pairs of house shoes and muddy boots neatly lined the closet floor. On the shelf at the top were shoe boxes that Maggie knew contained old tax documents and paperwork—she had seen them brought out in previous springs. Beside these boxes was a black plastic container about three inches deep. She hesitated, listening to the quiet house, then picked up the container and popped open the clasp on one side. Lifting the lid, she found a stethoscope, with its black tube and shiny metal pendant, the rubber pump of a blood pressure monitor, and the hard plastic tomahawk of a reflex tester. She placed the box on the top of the bureau and picked up the stethoscope, wondering whether her mother had needed these for giving birth at home, or for taking care of her own sick children, though Maggie had not seen the instruments before. The midwives had come, and the children had been sick in only ordinary ways and then taken to a doctor in town.

She placed the earpieces in her ears, wanting to hear the beat of her own heart, a childish impulse. When she slid the cold metal medallion between the buttons of her dress, she thought she heard someone approaching. She turned with sudden panic toward the bedroom door and in the moment before realizing that the sound she heard was her own heart beating, she had the sense that her imaginary grandmother had swooped into the room, cigarette in one hand and the other outstretched with ragged fingernails, demanding the doctor's kit. "Give me that," she hissed as Maggie pulled the stethoscope from her ears, "You're playing with grownup things."

Hands trembling, Maggie put the stethoscope into the box and placed the kit carefully back into the closet, closing the door. Though she crossed the floor in three wide steps, she felt like she was scrambling over the bed on her knees like a little girl, eluding the wrath of the grandmother, who everyone could see was not well. When the door to her parents' room clicked shut behind her, Maggie stood breathless in the children's room, letting her pumping heart slow. Downstairs, the screen door opened and shut: Douglas had returned to the house and was stopping at the kitchen sink for water. She listened to the tap run, the unfriendly territory of the house shrinking to enclose her.

CHAPTER SEVEN

When Maggie reached the kitchen a few moments later, Douglas was setting his glass on the counter and turning toward the back door. Their eyes met briefly, his face flushed, but he was preoccupied with his tasks and barely took notice of her. The screen door fell closed behind him.

In the pantry, she retrieved one of the knapsacks they used for grocery shopping to pack a lunch for later. She placed the book she'd brought down from upstairs at the bottom of the sack and on top of it packed the food that was easiest to carry: sourdough bread, cheese, a cucumber, an apple, and a sprig of cherry tomatoes. She was about to leave the kitchen when she caught sight of the open basement door and with a wave of concern remembered Lula. If she had forgotten the cat, even for a short time, what else had she neglected?

Maggie surveyed the empty dining room and living room, then went to the top of the basement stairs and called quietly for Lula. When the cat did not come, Maggie reluctantly descended the basement stairs, trying to ignore her old aversion for this dark space they so rarely used. She expected to see Lula lurking beneath the open wooden stairs without discretion, as if one place were as good as another, all equally without threat.

Reaching the bottom, Maggie stood on tiptoe to pull the chain for the naked bulb in the ceiling, which revealed only the washing machine and a small number of boxes—Christmas tree lights and baby clothes and unused canning supplies. Beside the boxes sat the heavy cherry crib that had been removed from the children's room. Here the concrete floor ran up against the mounds of dirt that then rose to the stone foundation of the house. To the right, the former owner had hung dark paneling from ceiling to floor in an unfinished attempt to make the basement feel less like the bottom of a dry well. Maggie listened hard for movement behind the walls, but heard nothing except the sound of her brother's feet shuffling against the floor above. She called again and waited. After a moment of silence, she turned and went back upstairs.

Maggie hesitated in the kitchen doorway, then went to Warren's bedroom door on the far side of the dining room table. She could not remember the last time she had knocked here, and she felt him inside, waiting for her as a guru waits on a mountaintop. The entrance to Warren's corner room was deeply inset into the wall. When she stepped into the brief passage, she felt for a moment as if she were entering her parents' bathroom one floor above.

"Come in," Warren said. He sounded more brisk and friendly than she might have expected, as if she were interrupting a small party rather than a long reading session.

When she entered, he sat facing her at his desk, the room lit by two windows, one on each wall. Here, too, the room looked just as she remembered—a twin bed pushed beneath the window looking out onto the side yard, a bookcase against the far wall lined with discarded library books, and the chair and desk to her right. "Have you seen the cat?" she asked.

Her brother absent-mindedly scanned the floor of his bedroom, as if the cat might have sneaked past his closed door. He was surfacing now from the joys of his reading, losing color, eyes dulling. "No," he said. "I've only been in here."

She nodded, hesitating. "I think Douglas might have let her out when he came in just now," she said. "Without realizing it. I've left the basement door open all the same."

He nodded, understanding that he should not close the door. He was so agreeable in his own way, so compliant, that she wanted to offer him something, the way she might Quinn or Edwin. "I've made some cold lunch," she said, holding up her bag. "To take outside with me for later. Should I bring you something before I go?" He never ate in his room but she could think of nothing else to suggest. "Some tea?" Her voice sounded a little too bright, as if she were imitating the receptionist.

Warren looked at her strangely. "I won't be hungry for a while," he said. His eyes wandered back to his text. Maggie turned to leave, then stopped and looked back. "On Monday I ate a cupcake given to me by a neighbor woman," she said. "The children call her the fat lady. She said you used to visit." She waited on his response, having asked a question without knowing quite what the question was.

He looked up from his book only slowly, as if the book were reality and she were a dream to be endured until waking. "Father forbids us to trespass on our neighbors' property."

"I was visiting," Maggie said, "which isn't the same as trespassing." She didn't mention that just yesterday they had all met in the rhododendron forest, yet no one suggested that anything was amiss.

"We're also not supposed to eat sweets."

Maggie did not immediately reply, feeling little concern over this rule she had broken. Living on her own must surely feel like this—a curious indifference to imperatives that no longer impacted her existence. After all, yesterday her father had given her permission to wander, and who knew whether he even remembered the other instructions from so long ago? Perhaps they'd been forgotten altogether.

"And yet the fat lady said you'd been there," she finally said.

"I've not done anything wrong," Warren said, sounding bored. "I went a time or two when I was younger, as did you and Phillip. We were with Mother." He pushed his fingers through the front of his hair, brow darkening beneath the shadow of his palm. " You'd do better to mind the rules yourself," he added, eyes drifting back to his book. "For everyone's sake." He had heard her upstairs, no doubt, and was warning her, though he would not tell their parents because to do so would be to pointlessly disrupt some hard-won peace. Afraid of crossing some boundary, Maggie did not ask whether he had eaten cupcakes with the receptionist the day before.

She was about to speak when from the kitchen the telephone rang, a hollow and disorienting sound. Warren's head snapped up.

Maggie stood in the doorway bewildered. She could not remember the last time the phone had rung.

The ring was sounding for a third time when Warren hissed, "Answer it." She looked at him, surprised, and then hastened to the kitchen. Of course the phone should be answered, and of course she should be the one to do so.

Picking up the phone felt so ominous that Maggie wondered whether there was in fact some ancient rule against it. In placing the receiver against her ear, she thought she heard a long, thin chuckle, followed by a man whispering, *Is your father home? I could sure use a favor.* But as she caught her breath, a familiar woman's voice much more clearly said, "This is a courtesy call from the public health department. Maggie, is that you?"

"Hello?" Maggie said.

"Hello indeed," the receptionist said, laughing. "Your mother should train you in some phone manners."

"I'm sorry," Maggie faltered. "We don't get many calls."

"Somehow that doesn't surprise me. I've called to check in on you. We try to do this with our patients. How are you feeling today?"

Maggie looked down at her bandage, which was soaking wet from washing clothes. She had not yet changed it. "My finger doesn't hurt today," she said.

"I'm glad to hear it," the receptionist said. "Be sure to keep the wound clean. And how's Lula?"

"She killed a rat last night," Maggie said warmly, glad she had good news to report.

"She works fast!" the receptionist said. "I must say I told you she would. I'll let you bring her home this weekend. Perhaps by then your father can be talked into getting one of his own. A barn cat."

"Yes m'am," Maggie said, hoping to appear better mannered. She did not remind the receptionist that since she was leaving in two days, she was not likely to be the one to return the cat.

"And what have you got planned for today?" the receptionist asked. Maggie could hear her filing her nails. Perhaps this is what Maggie and the witch would have done, had they remained friends, the witch examining the split ends of her long hair as they chatted about nothing on the phone. "This small rain shower is supposed to pass soon."

Maggie turned to look out the kitchen windows, realizing as she did that she could now hear the soft patter of drops on the tin roof, the kind that seemingly came from one cloud, leaving the rest of the sky sunny. "I'm—I'm not sure just yet," she said. With so little to offer, she mildly resented having to account for herself. "I'll read and eat lunch." The barn would be just the place to be out of the house and the rain.

"Perhaps you'll spend time with your brothers and sisters, since I'm sure they'll miss you when you go." The receptionist sounded farther away, as if she was cradling the phone in order to help a patient sign in.

"My family goes to the library on Wednesdays," Maggie said, not wanting to explain that as she had shared most of her life with her siblings, intentionally spending time with them now would feel unnecessary and strange.

"Well I've never met the youngest ones," the receptionist said. "I only remember Warren and Phillip. They played with my eldest boy a time or two. I've been thinking that I should talk your father into letting me borrow them for a day. I can't stay out from under these vines, and I'd like to pressure wash the porch. As a kindness for the cat, of course, and some pocket money. Wouldn't Phillip like to be paid for some chores?"

Maggie hesitated, feeling a familiar sense of privacy move within her like a guard stepping out on watch. "I suppose so," she said. Out the window Douglas was working through the rain shower, clipping the hedges. "Douglas likes to do that kind of work. He's almost fifteen."

"Hmmm. Well, I suppose anyone would do," the receptionist said. "Though I'd rather have an older boy. Perhaps I'll speak with your father about it. It would be such a huge favor for me."

A favor, the man's voice whispered again, clouding Maggie's thinking through the polite goodbyes. When she hung up the phone, she felt sluggish. The unusually large number of interactions with strangers over the last couple of days had drained her, dulled her, even, so that in turning away from the phone to assess the spring shower, she half expected to see melted snow dripping from the eaves of the house.

* * * *

Hours later, Maggie awoke in the loft of the barn to noises in the back yard. She scooted to the edge of her blanket to peer through the wide cracks in the slats. Her siblings were playing king of the mountain on the storm cellar, a lump of earth as tall as Maggie with a locked wooden door on the side. Agnes was standing on top of the cellar as the ice queen, hands raised as if casting a spell on the others, who were making a collective shushing noise as they climbed the grassy mound, pretending to struggle against a hard wind. It was recess, then. Maggie's job had been to structure this play time while her mother and Bertie napped before the last series of lessons, but the children hadn't really needed help with their games, so she had mostly sat beneath the tree reading, stepping in only when something went wrong and required negotiation. Now she felt uneasy: the children appeared unsupervised, their mother behaving as if Maggie was there and not there at the same time, monitoring the children with her usual diligence and napping in the barn and watching other people's babies in the city, all at once.

Agnes led her siblings from the hill, the game having changed. They disappeared into the shallow cedar grove at the edge of their property near the road, the one wooded area where Quinn would venture without fear of tramps. After eating her lunch, Maggie pulled the knapsack straps over her shoulders and climbed down the ladder, leaving the blanket in the loft. Once in the sunshine, she stretched and blinked, eyes adjusting to the bright afternoon light. Lula was nowhere to be seen and Douglas had also disappeared. Maggie turned to follow the children.

The path they had taken wound through the cedars toward an open space, though Maggie had stayed within the bounds of the yard for some years now, calling to her siblings from the top of the storm cellar when recess was over, a rare occasion for letting her voice rise above that of a courteous chiding. Now, coming into the clearing, she remembered just how perfect the cedar stand was for play, since the grove was still on their property, but hidden away from the grown-ups. On the far side, her sisters lounged in a large crocheted hammock suspended from three trees. The hammock twine had been tied in a number of different patterns. In some places it held tight and taut, and in others, as in the corner where Ellen sat, it dangled, making a nest around her. Agnes perched above her on the high side, fingers grasping the cord to keep from sliding.

The girls stopped talking and stared at Maggie. As on Monday, they appeared to require a moment's decision before accepting her into their reality, reluctantly and with a grudge.

"Where did this hammock come from?" Maggie said, approaching them. She had intended to be playful and warm, but the curious hammock distracted her.

"You've not left yet?" Agnes asked, picking at a fraying knot.

Maggie was startled. "I leave on Friday," she said.

Ellen put her fingers to her lips. "Shhh. We're in prison," she whispered, as if Maggie might cause their captors to return with her loud voice.

"Oh?" Maggie spoke more quietly. "And how did you end up there?" She looked around for the boys. Perhaps if Agnes would relent a bit they might allow her to play with them for awhile. She could remember how.

"Prison is boring," Agnes said, leaning forward and speaking directly to her little sister. "We really should change the game."

Ellen shook her head. "Then they won't play with us at all," she said. "And the rest of the game, after we get out of prison, can be quite fun."

Agnes rolled her eyes and leaned back into the hammock, hands still grasping the rope. "I don't think the game will go that way today," she said.

"Father made this hammock, didn't he?" Maggie asked, remembering a time when he had experimented with knots. He bought a book of instructions and cut up some rope that he used to practice knotting in the evenings while the others were reading. At that time, their mother still allowed him to smoke his pipe inside by the fire, and Maggie had needed to reassure Douglas that their father was not going to become a sailor and leave them for the sea. Instead, he was creating this hammock, which she had never really used, already too busy with caretaking.

"It's like you were never here," Agnes said, ignoring Maggie's question. Her sister had been gone all day yesterday, and yet suddenly she wanted to be a part of things. "You were never here, and now suddenly you are here, except soon you'll be leaving. It's really all rather pointless." There had been no supervision at recess, which might not have mattered, had Quinn's curiosity not been piqued by the cupcake wrapper in Maggie's dress pocket the night before. When Edwin asked Agnes for help in sneaking away with Quinn to the fat lady's house, Agnes agreed, bouncing the ball against the barn wall while Ellen made clover chains, making their mother believe they were all playing outside as usual, though Agnes understood their mother would have little reason to imagine the children doing anything else. There hadn't been much need for supervision at recess for some time, and surely Maggie knew this, which was why she had made no special effort to be there. Threats did not lurk in the back yard, or at the fat lady's house, or so Agnes had reassured herself, intuiting that her brothers would be just fine on their visit, would not be overly harassed by the fat lady, would never be found out by their father, and would not be frightened by the prowling man who lived upstairs and who stared at the girls from the uppermost window when they passed below.

And sure enough, the boys had returned triumphant, Quinn elated, Edwin happy to have initiated his older brother, no harm done. Still, Agnes could not help thinking she should not have let them go, that none of them should be in the habit of going, since on her last visit with Ellen, they had stepped off the front porch to see the man crouching in the long grasses of the front yard as if he were about to spring on them like a tiger. "Little girls with sticky fingers," he whispered. "Come here and let me show you something." They had run all the way home, and though Ellen begged to go back, Agnes refused.

Maggie squatted beside the hammock, picking up a stick to trace in the dust, hoping inattentiveness would slowly disarm Agnes. "What do you make of the cat?" she said.

"Pretty," Ellen said. "She's nice and fat."

Agnes said nothing. Maggie wanted to tell them about her trip to the receptionist's the day before—about the sparkling balloons and the mug full of sweet hot tea—but she did not want to lure the girls farther into the woods, to a place that might not be entirely safe. Instead she said, "I had a mermaid costume long ago." Beneath her hand the line through the dirt had taken the form of a fish fin. "Mother made it, I suppose."

She glanced up at her sisters, who stared back at her hopefully: if she could not tell them a story about themselves, perhaps she could tell one about herself. "Did either of you ever wear a mermaid costume?" Maggie asked. "Did the mermaid costume get handed down?"

Agnes looked away, disappointed. Her sister had no story to tell. Instead she was ever asking after inane objects—the mulberries, the hammock, a mermaid costume.

"We've never had any costumes at all," Ellen said, sighing.

"They're expensive," Agnes said. "And pointless." Maggie's presence was pointless, the mermaid story was pointless, costumes were pointless, playing war was pointless.

"We do have dolls, though," Ellen said, perking back up, remembering their game. "Waiting for us on top of the storm cellar. When the boys win the war, we'll be freed from prison. We'll cross the bridge into a happier place. They'll let us play dolls. That's how the game goes."

Before Maggie could reply, shouts emerged from the nearby woods, and an instant later, a familiar teenage boy came charging through the trees to skid to a stop before them on the dusty ground. Behind him, Douglas was also trying to give a warrior whoop, though as he was unaccustomed to this kind of display, his face seemed contorted by the effort to eke out sound. Maggie's two little brothers jogged along beside, wielding large sticks and breathing hard. The four boys had been intent on the prisoners—to threaten or to rescue them, some battle lost or won—and looked startled to see Maggie, who had not figured into this scenario at all, whose very presence seemed vast and formidable, for she was, Douglas thought, quite intimidating without making any effort—all of that irritating self-assurance, all of that firstborn certainty about her right to exist, her purpose on the planet.

Standing, Maggie saw immediately why her sister Agnes had yielded power in the game making: Douglas was playing with them, as was his old friend from town, who was a foot taller and at least fifteen now.

"Have you come to rescue us?" Agnes said sardonically to the group of boys, throwing her legs over the edge of the hammock to climb out. Ellen had to hold on in order not to be tossed to the ground.

No one replied. No one knew how to play the game with Maggie there, and no one was clever enough to match Agnes' bored irony, easing them from one reality to the other. Maggie felt a sudden, panicked need to tell Douglas that the neighbor boy must go home: the boys were too old to be playing with her smaller siblings. For a moment, as they all waited on her to speak, Agnes stared at her in hard hatred as if secretly hoping she would do just that, round them up and bring them in. Then she looked away again, and all that Maggie could see was Edwin with small scratches along his thin arms, longing to impress the bigger kid from town, and Quinn, staring at the dirt intently, attempting to correctly gauge the temperature of the group on this matter of Maggie's intrusion. The tall boy switched his stick on the ground, looking bored. In his sweat-soaked tee shirt, Douglas suddenly shivered.

"I've not seen you in quite some time," Maggie said to the neighbor boy, whose name she could no longer recall. "How is your mother?" She would at least remind him that she was an adult—that there were other adults nearby.

The tall boy shrugged, resistant. But Maggie stood silent, expecting an answer. "Fine," he finally said. She wanted to ask him why he had come here after so long an absence. She had a right to know.

"There's room on the hammock," Ellen said to Maggie, the only one inclined to continue the game, to reference its existence, even. "You can be a prisoner, too, if you'd like."

Maggie felt a sudden welling of gratitude for her youngest sister, whom she saw had a store of generosity that might leave her defenseless. After her strange tour through the empty house this morning and the disconcerting telephone call, Maggie had only wanted some company from her siblings. A little glimpse of the children's make-believe world before she left for the city. Some reassurance that she had played a role at all, or that the rituals would remain, as she somehow wanted them to, in some form. But even though she had not gotten those things, Ellen was trying make a place for her.

Still, Maggie knew that she did not belong here now. Both her imagination and her authority were dwindling, leaving her as neither child nor adult. She would have told the neighbor boy to leave, but she suddenly felt she was no longer in charge.

"Phillip and Warren will be expecting you back at the house soon," she said to her siblings, wanting to give them some kind of weapon, an excuse should they need one, a reminder to the neighbor boy that older brothers lurked inside whom he did not need to know were almost perpetually oblivious to their younger siblings.

Seeing that Maggie was leaving, Ellen announced, "You'll have to exit this world by the bridge!" She smiled and pointed, delighted to have somehow included her older sister in the game after all. Turning, Maggie saw a long board suspended from the tree branches by a series of knots, another project of their father's. The swinging bridge dangled above the ground by about a foot. When she obediently stepped on it, feeling she could do nothing more than comply with Ellen's command, the board came within an inch of the ground. It was a bridge over nothing and to nowhere, and she exited with little grace and some shame, clutching the thick cords as she tried to keep her balance.

CHAPTER EIGHT

The bridge delivered Maggie to the edge of the neighbors' corn-field, the stalks stubby on the far side of the split rail fence. She followed the property line accompanied by a kind of melancholy, resisting the temptation to look back on the world of children's play that she had in reality left long ago and now knew she could no longer visit. Within moments, the voices behind her faded completely.

The fence curved downhill and away from their house, quietly resting against the slope. In an open field just past the barn, Maggie turned, thinking she saw a flash of green light from the round window high in the western wall. She waited for it to return, but the glare of white clapboards made her eyes water. Perhaps she did not care to know anything more about the room behind the window, some inconsequential storage space for discarded costumes and old baby clothes.

When the cornfield gave way to woods, she climbed the fence to look for a comfortable place to read in the shade. In the weeds at the edge of the field, a large flock of vultures sat hunched and intent on a meal. Maggie walked toward them slowly to see whether they would scare. When she came close, they fluttered, changing position to face her while still feeding, opening up a vista of torn animal flesh, their pink necks bold against the black feathers of half-raised wings. She had never seen such a collection of birds before, and felt strangely diverted from her unwelcome isolation. The vultures seemed to be a reward for her decision to venture out into the world, as if this event had been staged for her as natural occurrences often were in books, where characters never explored the woods without spotting an owl or an otter. What was nature there for otherwise, except to loom and pulse in collective anarchy? Given the chance, the creatures would bring their appetites inside as the rat had done, leaving droppings and inviting disease, just as the cold came inside and then the humidity, ushering in mold, decay, and rot. Cut from the roots, the wood of the walls and floors of their house nevertheless still breathed with the wood beyond the walls, alive in its swelling and shrinking, just as the stones of the foundation had been gathered from the stones dotting the hillside, moved and arranged but otherwise remaining unchanged. The house might have simply emerged from the ground as saplings amid a rock pile, an organic life form that contained the members of the family within like small seeds in pods.

Maggie ignored a flutter of fear and got close enough to see that the animal the birds were eating had four legs and fur. A bobcat, perhaps, or an old dog. Her next step was finally too close, and so the birds rose heavily, of more or less one accord. They would roost nearby, wait for her to leave, then return. She wondered that they had been threatened by her at all. On an autumn walk with her father long ago, they had come upon a flock of wild turkeys that had not been scared off by them, as even at such a young age she assumed they would be, submitting to the dominant species. Instead she remembered now how the turkeys kept advancing. By the time she began crying and her father scooped her into his arms, the birds were mere feet away from them, looming and fussing loudly about the human intrusion into their territory. "Back off, you damned birds!" her father had shouted, waving one arm, then kicking his leg as he backed away from them. By the time he stooped to grab a stick, exposing her head to their beaks, they had stopped as if at an invisible fence.

She had been afraid, but she did not remember the incident with fear, causing her to wonder why she had forgotten it in the first place. If the story had been told and retold among family, celebrated as feats of courage by the father and daughter, would she have remembered it better?

She glanced once more at the carcass on the ground, then raised her gaze to the tree line. A path at the edge of the woods opened as the cedar trees deepened. In a clearing far beyond she could barely make out what appeared to be a large gray house. Long ago she might have heard her father mention this neighbor, who rented out his land for others to till; none of the farmers her father greeted in mending the fences would have been the owner. Perhaps then the owner lived there, in that flat stretch of valley. Warren would tell her not to trespass onto some stranger's property, but Warren did not seem to be burdened by the long hours that were causing Maggie to feel hostile even toward books. And what was it that her brother was afraid of? Of the knowledge that came from stepping outside the boundaries, nothing more. She skirted the dead animal and ducked beneath a tree branch.

The path appeared to grow longer as Maggie walked within the shadows, and for a time she felt she was coming no closer to the gray house. The tunnel through the trees resembled the dark culvert under the road that she had explored as a child, the path through the rhododendron forest she had bumped along in a wheelbarrow, the brick chute beneath the hemlock trees at the receptionist's house, the narrow staircase into the fat lady's basement kitchen, and some other forgotten passage that wormed its way along the spine of their house and into its heart. Boots pounding the dirt, Maggie breathed deeply the fragrance buried in the bark of the trees and without effort began picturing an old man's hands curling cedar beneath his pocket knife as he shaped the wood into a serving spoon. The image stayed with her until finally she emerged from the forest into the grassy front yard of the farmhouse, where she indeed saw such a man sitting in a lawn chair, shaving wood with a pocket knife. He looked up when he heard her approach, stared a moment from beneath his straw hat as if appraising her, then resumed whittling. She recognized the man from the book she had read as a child, the same book she asked the librarian about the day before.

After a moment she stepped across the grass toward the man, which she had surely done before, so familiar did his position in the chair appear, the sweep of the full front porch behind him, the tin roof glinting in the sun. A swarm of red wasps climbed along the peak of the roof and the cicada song surged, though it was barely June and too early for them to resonate so loudly. She was uncomfortably hot, suddenly, and unbuttoned the sleeves of her dress and rolled them above her elbows, as if she might begin snapping beans, something she had surely once done on these front steps, with the rattling sound of dishes coming through the kitchen window.

Across the yard a half-dozen wooden birds were impaled on sticks in the grass, their wings twirling in circles in the breeze. The man carved on.

"She'll be around the house," he said, and spit tobacco juice into the grass. "You can look for her or wait for her to come."

"What are the birds for?" Maggie asked.

"Moles," he said. "Keeps the moles away."

"How?"

He glanced up. He had a beak of a nose with a hard bump across the top, and he stared at her with watery blue eyes as if he had overestimated her, and now needed to reassess. "Wind makes the birds fly, creates a vibration. Moles think the vibration is people. Predators. A reason to stay away."

"Because moles are blind," she said, filling in the piece of information that she knew. The man was carving again. He didn't look up. He held the same degree of contempt for other people that her father did, yet she felt she could push her grandfather in a way that she could not push her father. She could force some sweetness if she tried.

"What are you making?" she said. He did not want to talk and this made her perverse. She was beginning to have some practice talking to people she didn't quite know these last two days, pretending she was right at home with the family and friends from the past who her parents had for some reason abandoned, or who had abandoned them. Warren knew the reason, or he would not have shushed her when she asked after their grandparents, would not have told her that her memories were merely scenes from books.

The man finally looked up at her again, then held the spoon beside his weathered face, as if to show her that it was a self-portrait, round and brown streaked with lines. Indeed, she thought that here was a man who would act as a void into which she could throw all of her projections, finding him mysterious or wise, content or simple, the dull surface of his face never reflecting the absurdity of her assumptions. She supposed his wife had once been comforted by this phenomenon and now would find it a horror.

From around the left side of the house an old woman in a floral housedress carried a gourd and a bucket. She climbed the far stairs to the porch without noticing Maggie. Into the bucket she dipped the hollow gourd that the man must have carved and then she poured water onto the first of many geraniums in hanging baskets around the edge of the porch. Maggie recognized her as well as her routine, a comfort and a bore, like the fat lady's baking and the receptionist's tea. They would each anticipate their chosen rituals with pleasure, forgetting that they had lost some of their richness and promise.

At the next flower pot, the woman finally spotted Maggie. She set down the bucket and gourd and wiped her hands on her skirt. Maggie saw that she hesitated to interrupt this activity, just as the old man found it difficult to stop carving. Without looking up, the old man called, "Lena!" The sound ripped through the heavy heat of the afternoon, then subsided. He wasn't one to waste words and yet he wasted one now, calling to his wife who was already on her way. She didn't look at him, but kept her eye on Maggie.

When the old man heard his wife's house shoes shuffle across the concrete of the front walk he stood, folded his pocket knife and the lawn chair, and disappeared around the corner of the house, trailing spirals of cedar. Maggie picked one up and held it to her nose, watching her grandmother approach. She could see that it was her grandmother because of how much the old woman looked like her father—deep set eyes, wide cheeks, thin lips. Clip-on earrings made of green glass sparkled beneath her soft white curls. Maggie, who also did not have her ears pierced, wondered how much they pinched. She thought of the receptionist's plum nails and the church director's pink high heels and the fat lady's red ruffled apron. Instead of going to shop for specific items, perhaps the women made trips to the store just for color, selecting purchases by shade rather than use—small tokens, passing fancies, bright spots for dreary days.

"How'd you come to be here?" her grandmother asked. Her tone was neutral, holding no promise and no suspicion.

Maggie glanced back. The stand of cedars blocked the view of the hill to the north and all but the smallest patch of corn. Late afternoon approached and spring surged toward summer with the rising heat, causing the corn to appear to waver.

"I was looking for a place to read," Maggie said, turning toward her grandmother. She looked past her to the side yard, where a big hackberry tree would drip sap onto the roof in the fall. "I remember the tire swing," she said. "I once recited a lovely poem there, one that mother made me memorize." When had her mother ceased to require them to memorize poems?

"The one about the river," her grandmother said without any particular emotion.

"Yes, the river that travels to the sea," Maggie said, unsure of the nature of this unexpected homecoming, either for herself or for her grandmother. It hardly seemed a topic to approach directly, if at all. "Your flowers look nice."

The grandmother turned to look at the porch. "They do, don't they? I so rarely look at them from this angle. I'd have to come out here and turn around, as if I was arriving and would leave again, and that doesn't seem wise, somehow." Maggie said nothing, but thought of the window hanging like a moon in the corner of her own house that she had noticed only because she'd arrived like a stranger, knowing she'd leave again soon.

Her grandmother shuffled back toward the front stairs. "You may as well come on inside," she said. "I'll finish the flowers later. We won't eat supper for another hour or two, but you'll want a snack, I suspect, as children do."

For a moment after Maggie entered the wide hallway she saw people grouped around tables eating and laughing and opening gifts. Then the vision faded and the hall was quiet. The doors to the rooms on each side were open, letting sunlight into the otherwise dimly lit hallway that was filled with furniture—a desk, a china press crammed with knick knacks—the clutter a relief after the more empty houses of the neighbors. Maggie saw the swirl of a red sheer curtain in her grandmother's bedroom briefly before they passed, and heard muted television voices from the other side of the hall. The house was like a child's drawing of a butterfly, the hallway the body and the four rooms the wings. At the second door on the left they entered the kitchen.

From the refrigerator, her grandmother pulled leftovers—macaroni and cheese, chocolate pudding, fried okra, slices of ham. She pointed to the kitchen cabinet where Maggie could see a coconut cake and a glass jar filled with chocolate and peanut butter balls. Then she said, "Heat anything you want in the toaster oven. Leave the food out when you're finished since we'll eat soon enough.

Now if you'll excuse me, the stories are on. You never much cared
for soap operas when you were little, and I can't imagine that would
change just because you're older."

She left the room. Through the doorway from the kitchen to the
living room, Maggie could hear her settle with a squeak into what
must have been a leather chair. She wondered for a moment if this
was her imaginary grandmother, the one who once owned the round
box, but they did not seem to look or act the same. She retrieved a
spoon from the drain board to dip directly into the leftover pudding
bowl, intending to eat it all, then poured herself a glass of milk from
the refrigerator, which was filled with other containers covered with
plastic, bits of leftovers the old couple were working on. Then she
settled herself at the table. The pudding was almost without flavor,
yet still pleasantly cold against her tongue. She was becoming a con-
noisseur of sweets simply by visiting her neighbors, and she hoped
that the church in the city did not forbid desserts, as she could now
not quite imagine an existence without them.

From where she was seated, Maggie could just see the chicken
coop. Her grandfather had set up his whittling there by the wire fence.
Beyond, a gravel road wound toward the house and then away again.
If she had come here as a child with her family, as of course she had,
they must have arrived by the road, bringing casserole dishes and
bags full of baby supplies.

Maggie thought maybe she felt warmly toward these surroundings,
which held comfort and some connection with people gathering to
exchange information and stories. She closed her eyes, summoning
the same sensations she had remembered at the library the day before:
a smooth brown egg in her palm, the ticklish asparagus frond, a

swirl of muddy pond water, cow dung buzzing with flies. And yet suddenly she opened them again, feeling as though she had been moving carelessly through the dark, making herself vulnerable to small injuries—the tear of barbed wire, the invisible needles of the prickly pear, the tug of tweezers against an embedded tick, and then something beyond all of that which had no material form. She finished her pudding quickly, left the bowl in the bottom of the sink, and walked softly to the living room doorway.

In the armchair her grandmother slept, head tilted back and mouth open, emitting a light snore. Across the room, her grandfather's matching chair was positioned with a spittoon on one side and an end table with a Bible on the other. The Bible waited to be opened, while the black phone on the far wall waited to ring, a party line that her grandmother had to share with another neighbor just as Maggie's family did at home. Between their chairs the ceramic gas grate was cold and pale. On the television a woman was crying, gripping the shoulders of a man who towered above her. Watching them, Maggie remembered warning her grandmother against these stories, sensing their power to create longings that might not otherwise exist, which Maggie had then understood better than anyone. "You'll not want to watch those shows, Grandmother," she had chided, barely looking up from a book that she could not put down, so much did she want to live in the world of the heroine, who had a hideout, a group of friends who were not family, and interesting problems to solve. Her grandmother often spoke of heaven as a peaceful place, but Maggie had hoped that the after-life would consist of enacting for eternity the kinds of stories she was then reading, in which all of the conflict was external to the workings of the world, resolvable either with immediate action or reasonable, sympathetic conversation.

"You'll want to show more respect for your elders," her grandmother snapped, but Maggie did not pay her any mind, reading on as a barricade against the ocean swell of silence that might otherwise swallow her on this Sunday afternoon visit, no less in this house than in her own. For she had remembered the book correctly, and though a pleasant enough place to visit, not much had happened here. After the last two days of unexpected conversations, Maggie felt she had again dipped into the same disorienting silence of childhood, a silence that, like laughter, later kept you from remembering any of the particulars of what had been funny in the first place, the emotion so consuming as to momentarily free you from the act of recording. Closing her eyes, she breathed deeply in unison with her grandmother, listening from sleep for the crunch of tires on the gravel road or the thud of horse hooves against the dried dirt, sounds which never came. From the open windows she felt the dry wind that would not bring rain. Outside tonight, the foxes might draw close to the hen house with their short screams. A shiftless stranger might walk across the front porch in the moonlight, rousing her grandfather to retrieve his rifle. The drought would press in, draining the barrels of rainwater for the geraniums. For now, the silence gathered like heat, lulling them all with the illusion of safety, as they burrowed and slept beneath its weight.

Maggie opened her eyes again. She should not linger here any longer. Unable to politely take her leave until her grandmother awakened, she felt again as she had when trapped in the witch's bedroom all those years ago, torn between places. Maggie could not think what other place she might prefer to be now. At a loss, she wandered into the bedroom across the hall where she climbed onto a high wrought iron bed, sluggish in spite of her earlier nap. She took a magazine from the nightstand, propping it on the pillows. It was a familiar religious publication of her grandmother's, many years old. Maggie's favorite part had been one column at the edge of the page that told a story about how God worked mysteriously, always in defiance of the laws of nature. In this particular issue, the magazine retold a story from the early days of colonization that Maggie remembered having read before. A panther had caught a pioneer woman in its mouth and taken her up into a tree. He would have eaten her had she not sang hymns all night long, soothing the panther the way that David had soothed Saul with his harp in the Bible, until her family, come looking for her, had shot the panther. The woman was saved, which indicated that God was just. Although the rest of the articles in the magazine suggested that most dangers came from the spiritual world, this story surely was strong evidence that the material world provided the real terrors—the incidents that occurred without warning or reason. No dramatic event had ever happened to her family, and yet surely something must have threatened them into behaving with such an exaggerated degree of caution.

Maggie had been dozing for quite some time when she awakened to a harsh whisper coming from the kitchen. "Hush up, you," her grandmother hissed. "You'll not talk to me with your foul mouth." Then she began to sing words from a hymn that Maggie recognized, as if she, too, had a panther to keep at bay. Maggie sat up in the bed, noticing that the room had grown dim while she slept. Her grandmother began to sing, *Jesus is on the main line.* Through the window, Maggie saw her grandfather walking in the garden with bent neck, examining the tomato plants. The sound of the television was gone, but a table fan whirred from the kitchen between lines from the song and the refrigerator gurgled, chirruping like a squirrel. "I won't say your horrid swear words," her grandmother said, and Maggie imagined that she was addressing the animated appliance. "No matter how bad I feel."

Maggie felt a small chill. She had let her attention lapse. She had been gone from home too long, and she needed more than anything to check on Lula. It had grown late, and her grandmother, who had admittedly been welcoming only to a point, was now talking to herself in agitated tones, as if resisting the onset of an evening transformation.

Maggie slid off the bed just as she heard her grandmother's steps in the hallway, then the half-closed bedroom door swung open. Standing in the entry, her grandmother appeared relaxed. Her face was soft and puffy, and she wore a gentle smile. "Did you rest well?" she asked.

"Yes," Maggie answered. "I'm sorry. I think I've overstayed my welcome. I'll have to be getting home now," she glanced out of the window, "before dark."

Her grandmother's eyebrows arched. "Smooth over your bed first," she said. "Then come to the kitchen to help with the dish washing before you go." She turned, leaving the door open. Maggie looked at the bed. She had unsettled the lacey throw pillows that leaned against the larger pillows covered with pink satin shams. She righted the pillows, smoothed the creases in the comforter, and tugged at the top corner to make the hem hang straight at the base of the bed. She walked quickly to the kitchen, uneasy about the dark in a way that she had not been at the fat lady's, since she was farther from home, in less familiar territory.

Her grandmother stood at the kitchen sink, filling the left side with steaming water, soap suds rising around a stack of dishes. On the counter a tall pile of empty glass and plastic bowls awaited washing. The leftovers themselves were piled onto a large serving platter in the middle of the kitchen table, presumably for when her grandfather came in for supper.

In penance for eating all of the pudding and for appearing out of nowhere on a Wednesday afternoon to disturb her grandparents' hard-won peace in isolation from their son's family, Maggie began to rinse the dishes and listen to her grandmother talk. "I might have had girls, too," Lena said briskly, the warmth replaced with the clipped speech appropriate to performing a task. "Someone to talk to. But I only had one boy. The girls I was supposed to have I lost. After my miscarriages, the doctor came to the house to scrape out my insides. To prevent infection. They did that, then—house visits. No chloroform or anything." She rubbed the wash cloth against a resistant bit of egg on a plate. She was telling a story that she had told before, which brought her no relief. Maggie had thought that stories might help define, record, and liberate, but listening to her grandmother now, she was not so sure. "I'm a Methodist. I don't drink or smoke. I don't swear. How's one to find comfort? In the Lord? I'm a Methodist," she said again. "I look for comfort in the Lord. The Lord is my lover, friend, and guide." She looked out the window to where her husband was now coming around the house. He climbed the stairs and eased onto the porch swing, spitting tobacco juice into the grass. "Do you suppose that business of scraping the insides is really even all that necessary?" she glanced at Maggie. "I always think I might have been all right without it."

Maggie felt as if her own insides were shrinking, tensed against intrusion. She did not know how to reply. She had read many books in which grandmothers told granddaughters stories about the old days while they completed some task together, like hanging newly washed sheets from the line, the laundry bright and billowing in the sun unlike the dull dress she had left dragging to dry this morning. These grandmothers offered their granddaughters bits of wisdom as asides, lessons told craftily in order that their granddaughters would absorb and remember these important truths. These were the same grandmothers who kept trunks full of curios and small treasures in the attic, while in this house, such a trunk would be filled with old towels cut into rags. Here, no one kept a diary or took photographs or wrote letters to kin that mimicked the sentiments from their reading, obscuring the pain of stillbirth or the relentless sameness of the work.

"Do you want babies?" her grandmother asked suddenly.

Maggie hesitated. "I leave for the city on Friday, where I'll work in the church nursery," she said. This seemed the most polite way of saying no.

Lena nodded. "Best not to have them if you don't want them," she said. "For those that have babies, girls are the key. You must have someone to talk to." She nodded toward the man in the swing. "Useless," she said about her husband. "How is it possible to say so little? What are his thoughts like? I believe that it's possible that he thinks only in pictures—no words—only of what's in front of him. He sees what's happening to the plants and to his wood carvings. Sometimes I think I'll forget words. Without the television and the Bible, I probably would."

Her grandmother pointed with a dripping plastic yellow glove to the wooden trellises covered in budding rose bushes against the fence at the edge of the yard. "He built me those," she said. "It's the kind of thing he's good for. I make his meals. It's the kind of thing I'm good for."

"Didn't your son talk with you?" Maggie was unsure how to ask this question, not knowing whether she should reference her own father.

"Now there's a question. Do you chat with your father?" her grandmother asked with a wry smile.

"Not really, no."

Lena looked satisfied, perhaps relieved that the world was as she thought it to be. "Your father did use to share with me. He could be quite the talker. But they grow out of it, the men in our family."

"And so perhaps my father—"

"You'll not want to mention your father here, dear," her grandmother said as if Maggie was the one who had introduced her father into the conversation. "It makes your grandfather very upset."

The stack of dishes slowly grew smaller, as the dark fell outside. When the last dish was washed, Maggie dried her hands on a towel. The bandage for the rat bite was soaked and so she pulled it off and put it in her pocket.

"What happened to your finger?" her grandmother asked, pulling off her rubber gloves.

Maggie hesitated. "A rat bit it," she said, "while I slept the other night."

"Now there's a problem we've never had here," Lena said, reaching out to examine Maggie's finger. Her pinky was wrinkled, the puncture marks red but not inflamed. "Mice, yes, but no rats—not in the house." She dropped Maggie's hand and turned toward the pantry.

In a moment she was back with some gauze and tape. "Barn cats is what you need," she said, bandaging the finger.

"We've got a cat now. She killed a rat just this morning."

"Ah?" Lena said, wrapping the bandage around Maggie's finger. "Your father never could abide by pets—not in the house. He's a good farm boy in that way if no other. Cats are for the barn, dogs are for the yard. What good are they otherwise?"

"She's a lend from a neighbor," Maggie said.

"That sounds right," her grandmother said, tucking the tape into her pocket.

"When I get home, I'll have to make sure that she's been properly fed." Maggie turned to pick up her bag from the kitchen chair, unsure of how best to make her departure. "Thank you very much for a lovely afternoon." She spoke as if she had called for tea time with a play-mate. She had no other, more natural phrases suited for an occasion in which she had spoken at length with a long-lost grandmother without even discovering why she had been lost in the first place. "I must be going now." She pulled the straps across her shoulders.

"That's quite a big book you've got there," her grandmother said, placing her hands on her hips. "And to think it's all about rabbits."

Maggie kept her eyes on the strap that she was untwisting, trying not to reveal any alarm that her grandmother had opened her pack. What intuition told her subtlety was best? Did everyone behave so in uncertain circumstances? She thought she heard a whisper, and for an instant she was back in the room across the hall, a much smaller girl clutching a red leather book in her hands, her grandmother leaning over to say, "Can't you share what you've written in your diary with your Granny?" But in the kitchen, her grandmother was simply saying, "I've put some peanut butter balls down inside in a paper bag."

"Thank you," Maggie said, chastising herself for mistrusting her grandmother. Then she looked out at the dark and felt the doubt return—she must look to herself, get on home.

She turned toward the front door, and her grandmother followed. "Of course you're welcome to stay overnight, if you don't think your family will miss you," she said casually.

"The cat—" Maggie said. "And then I must also get ready to leave for my job. Tomorrow is my last day at home."

"Your job in the city, yes, I know." Her grandmother held the door that Maggie had opened, then gestured for her to open the screen door. "You speak of it as if it's a destiny. But it's just a job." She paused, turning on the porch light. "What does your mother say to your going?"

Maggie said nothing at first, coming to a standstill on the porch. She turned to face her grandmother, who stood with the screen door closed behind her. "I suppose she doesn't like it," she said, wondering if this meant that her mother would miss her.

"Naturally she needs you at home," her grandmother said as if answering this question. "There's a neighbor who sometimes tells me of your younger siblings. All of those little ones I've never met."

"They're old enough now," Maggie said, meaning that her grandmother might meet them if she wanted to. She was impatient to leave, tired of the ways that other people hemmed themselves in, then expected her to honor the arbitrary boundaries they created. She did not know why her grandparents no longer spoke to their son or the rest of the family. She did not need to know in order to guess that the reason would be childish, trivial.

"And the rooms at your house—they're rather crowded these days? A good enough reason to leave as any."

Maggie shrugged. "I suppose so." Out beyond the porch the cicadas were raging.

"Your father understands the limits to what's in the city. Family is a bigger obligation than what you think. That's the lesson he learned long ago."

"That he should not leave, you mean?" Maggie asked, remembering the witch saying her father once wanted to leave but could not.

"Yes. Staying is better. The same lesson you'll be learning, if you leave. Except that if you return, you might find that the place won't welcome you back. It's a risk you should consider." Her grandmother reached over to pluck a dead bud from a pot of geraniums set on the porch floor. "Here you'd have a big room of your own. A television and radio. I'll teach you to bake. Give you a spot in the garden. You can visit your family so long as you don't talk about them with us."

Maggie's father had wanted to be elsewhere all of these years, and her mother had been elsewhere, roaming foreign terrain from the comfort of the house. Yet when Maggie had decided to leave two days ago she'd not been congratulated nor designated an ambassador for the family. As compensation, she should feel that her parents wanted her there with them. But she was not at all sure that they wanted her. The receptionist had seemed to want her, but the receptionist wanted other things more—wanted her son back, for instance. In contrast, her grandmother now seemed to want her. She had asked for her and laid out the terms of engagement explicitly. Maggie could easily enough imagine having the big room with the high bed all to herself and having the attention of her grandmother—however twisted and soured—all to herself. She would take on the responsibility of watching over her grandparents as she had done for the children, as she would soon be doing for other people's children in a place where no one knew her. What advantage did one place have over another?

"That sounds lovely," Maggie whispered, for she was heart-sick. "Thank you for the invitation." She hesitated, staring into the darkness that surrounded them now, waiting for one more signal from her grandmother, something which might tip the balance. After all, Lena had wanted to punish her for coming, wanted her to stay one night, and wanted her to stay for good, all in the space of a couple of hours. Hadn't she?

"You're free to go, of course," her grandmother said with a touch of scorn as Maggie hovered at the top stair. And in the counter-intuitive way of such reassurances, Maggie saw that she hadn't been free to go for quite some time, and that she might not be free to go come Friday. The church in the city reared up in her mind as an oasis, breathing its people in and out, in and out. She quickly turned to descend the stairs.

"No more visits now, darling," her grandmother said. Looking back, Maggie saw Lena's white hair glowing in the porch light that had begun attracting moths. Her grandmother was peering out into the dark, as if wondering what else the world might heave onto her front steps, and how long she would have to wait for it. "You've upset your grandfather. If you come back, you'll come only to stay."

Without saying goodbye, Maggie began to walk toward the stand of cedars. Later at home, she would tell Warren about this place so she would not forget it again. She would get up the courage to ask him what he knew.

"Be careful," her grandmother called from behind her. "The tramps come out after dusk."

CHAPTER NINE

During the book conversation following Wednesday night's dinner, Warren listened for the cat that was lurking somewhere in the house, just as that morning he had listened to Maggie enter their parents' room for reasons he could not fathom. After Maggie left, he had simply gone back to reading, not at all concerned about the cat's whereabouts—she would turn up somewhere, sometime. Now that the afternoon had passed without his seeing her, without his hearing one of the children coo over her or his mother exclaim at her appearance, he wished he'd been more attentive. A cat as affable as this one would not under usual circumstances stay out of sight for so long. Surely soon some scratch or plaintive meow would alert the others to the hidden space at the center of the house, a collective recognition he did not think they would be able to ignore.

In every other way the evening was ordinary, with Warren sitting at the dining room table with the children, showing interest in their book selections as if that was indeed what their father would have done were he there. Their mother knitted from the rocking chair beside the wood stove, a quiet smile on her face as if her life's work had been preparing her children for these halting literary discussions. In the living room, Phillip read a biography with his leg slung over their father's armchair, a small transgression speaking to the weekly relief from paternal patrol. Douglas stretched along the couch, still wearing his sweaty tee shirt in an effort to distinguish himself, waiting to shower at a time that would inconvenience the others, interrupting nightly routines.

For now, the children were excited by the library's acquisition of a new series for their age group that Agnes, as the eldest, would get to read before the others.

"The librarian said we were the first kids to check out the new books," Edwin said proudly, eyeing the stack of three beneath Agnes' neatly folded hands. They were all nervous: if Agnes liked a book, she would immediately begin rereading it, especially if it made her cry or scared her.

"But we've only got them for three weeks," Ellen said with a hint of worry. "Because they're new. We can't renew them. There will be a waiting list, she said."

Edwin shot Ellen a look. If they provoked Agnes by rushing her in any way, asking what page she was on now, she would abuse her power and take longer than ever to finish. For the moment, however, Agnes seemed unruffled, content in her rights.

Warren teased Ellen, saying, "The characters in those books will keep doing whatever it is that they are doing. They won't stop before it's your turn."

"And the ending will remain the same?" Ellen said. "No matter who is reading it?"

"Nothing changes no matter who is reading," Warren replied.

Ellen sighed. After a moment of silence, she said quietly, "Even for the neighbor boy, I suppose. Though he is so bossy and treats the rest of us like babies."

The room fell still in discomfort at Ellen's feelings, so clearly stated for everyone to hear. Douglas lay like a corpse on the couch. Their mother, who over dinner had seemed pleased to discover that Douglas' old playmate had stopped by, ceased her slow rocking. Agnes' hands remained tightly clasped across the coveted books. Only Phillip read on, apparently oblivious, while Bertie's red crayon took a nosedive across the page.

"Even for him," Warren said reluctantly. Having seen Maggie follow the children into the woods earlier, Warren had given up whatever small responsibility for them that he felt in the shifting rules since her announced departure. There was no need for worry. The yard was safe. The woods were safe. And no one came to visit anymore. But then today this playmate had suddenly returned—for what?—had returned to play with Douglas after long absence. Warren assumed some wound had healed and made new discourse possible.

Ellen was frowning. Wanting to comfort her, Warren added, "Although perhaps I am wrong, and characters do perform better for some than for others. Perhaps when they're not fond of a particular reader, they simply lie down on the page and refuse to participate."

Ellen giggled, pleased to be indulged with whimsy. She pictured the strange neighbor boy puzzling over a story in which the main character had curled up for a long nap or drifted off the page to wait in the margins for a better reader. Satisfied, she handed Warren one of her picture books to read aloud.

Agnes, however, did not brighten. She had in fact been quite intimidated by the boy, if only because he had not understood their family's rules—that their sister's underwear drying on the clothes

line should not be mentioned, that their brother's long runs did not
bear examination (where's the race? the boy had asked), that their
homeschooling was both sensible and natural, since their mother
knew more than all the local teachers combined.

And yet the boy had caused her a tremor of dread as early as this
morning, when on the trip to the library the family stopped off to
chat with his mother. Agnes was afraid that without Maggie, the
women along the street would speak with less warmth and for less
time, her family's feeble connection to the outside world threatened
by their mother's struggle to appear approachable, to not walk as
if others had the measure of her worth or she had the measure of
theirs. To her surprise, however, as the family came upon the woman
sweeping her walkway, their mother stepped up to the fence without
hesitation, calling her greeting.

"I hope Maggie isn't sick?" the neighbor said as she set down her
broom and approached them.

Their mother shook her head. "She's taken childcare work in the
city." She spoke without the shade of reproof that Agnes might have
expected. "She's home getting ready to leave."

"I see." The woman glanced at the faces of the children as if to
discern what this news might mean to them. "You all will miss her,
I expect."

"It will be harder, getting along without her," their mother said,
as if Maggie were an old and dear servant, which of course in some
ways she was. "But she'll do a good job there, and after all, it was
time." Agnes again felt a wave of resentment, fearing that Maggie's
abandonment had created some looming risk for them all, a suspicion that was confirmed when she looked up to see the pale face of

Douglas' friend in the upstairs window, watching them just as the fat lady's companion had.

"I'm sorry to see her go," the boy's mother said. "And where is Douglas today?"

"He's stayed home to do chores. Yard work. Something he took a liking to last year." Their mother spoke in an understated tone, Agnes noticed, as if Douglas routinely missed their trip to the library to work alone, and yet she could see that her mother glowed. "He has a knack for it," she said, shrugging slightly, as if she might have it otherwise. Agnes had not heard her mother say so much to anyone outside the family in years. For a moment she had the disorienting sense that it was Maggie who, like a domineering husband, had kept their mother in her place.

"I'm glad to hear it," the woman said. "Boys need to be active. Need work to do." She glanced with a frown toward the house as if suddenly wondering what her own son was up to, then turned back to say goodbye, smiling again. Still, the woman must have seen what Agnes had seen, which was that Maggie was already lost to the city and Douglas the new favored project. And yet to what end? Their mother had not cared whether the yard was overgrown in years and had given up on the vegetable garden long ago. Surely then she was planning something, and indeed when the pianist and the gardener and the others made their own inquiries, her mother's replies were spoken with the same measured enthusiasm that no one need suspect or recoil from, a seed planted for some other season. Douglas might even become a novelty, a member of the family to enter local commerce where his older brothers had failed, granting some employer access to a family otherwise so removed, with their secrets still kept.

Yet of course they had nothing to hide.

Listening to Warren now read about a talking frog, however, Agnes thought that perhaps there was something hidden here after all—something he now turned over with part of his mind, since the dialogue was coming out wrong, the punctuation rushed. He flushed slightly. She watched, curious about the source of the emotion flitting across his face that the children did not notice. Then she looked away: she was bored with her older siblings' preoccupations, whatever they might be, just as she was bored with the younger kids' story, and ready to read her own.

Warren began coughing loudly. "I'm afraid something is tickling my throat," he said. He reached for the water pitcher in the center of the table, coughing all the while, for he had heard a faint scratching sound coming from his bedroom wall and was desperate to cover it up. "Perhaps we should end here."

The children did not complain, having grown restless with the desire to read on their own. As they scattered he rose clumsily, scraping the heavy bench loudly across the floor.

One moment later and Warren stood breathless behind his closed bedroom door, listening as the cat explored the staircase hidden between the walls of his bedroom and the dining room. With each scratching sound, his fear reached a new peak, as if this space behind the wall that he had only ever imagined was his own secret about to be revealed. From beyond his bedroom door, however, he could hear no changes—a page turned, the rocking chair squeaked. Their mother cleared her throat. She was the only other one in the household with some ancient and abstract awareness of the staircase, keeping the knowledge so carefully guarded that she would be devastated by its appearance after all of these years. He on the other hand understood intuitively and then from study that the stairs led from the basement below to the back of the pantry, and then on up to a room above that couldn't be much bigger than the bathroom that it was hidden behind. He had never seen the upstairs room or the narrow staircase, yet after years of listening, he knew that the back of the pantry had at some time been covered in sheetrock, cutting off access to the stairwell from the ground floor, but leaving entrance to the second floor and the basement. Behind the wood paneling in the basement, the foot of the staircase met up with the underground passage that led to the storm cellar. Someone—a servant presumably—could restock the pantry without ever venturing outside.

Whoever that servant had been. Warren had come to imagine a middle-aged man waiting on an eccentric elderly man who was wealthy enough to pay for company and care, but who desired nothing else—this was not a grand house for entertaining, after all, but an awkward one, with rooms perhaps filled with relatives who did not want to be concerned with their kinsman's illness, just as he did not want them interfering with his health, hovering about in expectation of inheritance.

This vision of the previous owner's arrangement came when Warren was older, however, since the first time he heard a light tread move unaccountably down and through the walls, he assumed the house was haunted—did ghosts have footsteps in spite of being weightless? Was that part of their menace, this incongruity? At that time he had already been sleeping peaceably in the downstairs room for months or years, perhaps—ever since age eight, when the babies filled the nursery and his younger brother was old enough to take up his own place off the living room, sometimes awakening Warren when he was too scared to sleep alone. Terrified by the sound of someone coming or going at regular intervals, Warren struggled to picture the material world grounding the movement he heard. This would take some practice, though in truth, even as an adult he was never sure he could grasp the material world grounding existence. Always it was as if he were reaching beyond it, down long dark shafts to find the mechanism for its operation.

One night Warren waited for the noises to stop, then climbed the stairs and entered the nursery, where Douglas, Agnes, Ellen, and Quinn slept soundly in the shimmering light from the window. He did not usually come to his parents' room because his father said they had enough to do with interruptions from the little ones, but he felt sure that his parents would want to know that he'd heard an intruder. It was, after all, his responsibility to be the man of the first floor of the house as he had been told, and so his father would be proud of him for neither sleeping nor crying like a baby. The door was partly open and so it was easy to slip inside.

In the dark he stood at the foot of the bed, waiting. After a moment his mother awoke and pushed herself up on her elbow. "What is it, sweetheart?" she said, for she still said such things back then.

Warren looked to his father's side of the bed. Though he intended to wake his mother first, it was his father that he must tell. But his father's place was empty. His mother looked over her shoulder at the indented pillow and creased sheets, then glanced at the dark crack at the base of the closed bathroom door. After a moment's pause in which she seemed to consider a new piece of information, she turned back to Warren and said, "Your father's out in the shed smoking his pipe. A nasty habit I hope you'll never imitate." She waited for him to say why he had come, and when he did not, said, "Weren't you sleeping well?"

Warren shook his head. What could he say but that he had heard a noise that he now realized was his father, and been scared for them all? He would look like a coward.

His mother, already retreating into the small space she would create for herself in her mind, kindly told him to go back to bed. "Try to get some sleep," she said, dismissing him without a parting kiss. But then perhaps he underestimated her. Perhaps she had been alarmed at the possibility that he would remain awake long enough for his father's return, and so she did not summon him to the bedside for a kiss but simply waited as he turned and crept back out of the room. When the heavy steps came again sometime later, Warren was wide awake. Smoking a pipe, then, was such an extraordinary evil that it required a secret advance and retreat.

From then on, his father had two selves—stern and solid in the daytime, and fluid, omnipresent, and roaming at night, with clouds of pipe smoke trailing behind him. The noises occurred more and more frequently until at some point they died out altogether, as all things did, the ground thawing into a spring of such voracious appetite that the vegetation overstepped its limits, with vine over vine amassing until death sprouted from the tight dark center. In the morning, the alternate identity receded with the dark. In the morning, all was as it should be, which was so little of what anyone ever wanted. Long after the night noises stopped, Warren puzzled over the pattern of sounds, poring over architecture books in what his mother would call his junior high reading obsession, after which he would abandon the concrete for the abstract. He had come to understand what he needed to: a servant's staircase, a cellar door, and a round upstairs window that the other children had learned to ignore long ago on his instruction. His father desired not to overtly disturb either his wife or the children, avoiding their sleeping innocence at the expense of just one child, the one who occupied this room below.

The cat seemed to have moved on. Warren sat at the edge of his bed to wait for everyone to retire, his undershirt wet with sweat. He heard his mother dismiss the younger children, who filed through the bathroom then followed her upstairs. Douglas started the shower and Phillip retreated to his room. Upstairs the springs of their parents' mattress squeaked, the sound that in recent years Warren rarely had to block with a pillow over his head. He sometimes had the queasy sense that he might be able to pinpoint the night Bertie had come into being, the same night that his own nascent longings had been obliterated forever, or so it sometimes seemed. He wondered if Phillip could tell this about him, as if his brother was listening at doors, sniffing him over breakfast, sensitive to the absence of the activity that Phillip pretended he had in abundance outside the confines of the house.

Finally Warren rose, slipped from his room, and crossed through to the kitchen. At the basement door he stopped, hoping the cat would hear him and run up the stairs of her own accord, for he did not believe she was actually trapped. When she did not do so, he descended into the dark, careful to pull the door closed behind him. He did not want her to run out without his seeing her. At the bottom of the stairs, he felt for the long string hanging from the ceiling and turned on the bulb, his eyes adjusting to the bright light as he surveyed the basement. When he didn't see the cat, he approached the wood paneling on the south end and bent down to where it nearly met the floor. How had she slipped beneath? His eyes followed the pressed wood along the floor and up the mound of dirt toward the foundation of the house, where the clay created a lumpy tabletop. Here, where the dirt did not meet the straight cut of the pressed wood, there was a gap large enough for a small animal. Warren leaned into its cold dampness and called to her very quietly. He had never called a cat before and felt how forced and unnatural he sounded. He had no relationship to this cat. He could not remember her name.

"Kitty?" he whispered. He waited, not hearing even a rustle. After a moment, he retreated to the kitchen and filled her shallow bowl with fresh water. He set the water on the top of the basement stairs along with the tough end of a ham, leaving the door cracked. He did not know what else to do to protect their mother, and in a wave of bitter blame, felt he would not be suffering in this way if Maggie had not been breaking the rules as if there were no consequences— wandering in the woods, visiting their neighbors, sneaking into their parents' room, neglecting the children and the cat. She could leave soon enough if she wanted to, but the rest of them would have to live with whatever turmoil she created with her selfish mistakes.

He turned out the kitchen light to go to bed, then hesitated. The phone hung in the shadows, a menace he had forgotten until this afternoon. When it'd rung, he felt some disproportionate dread he could not name and quickly returned to reading to be rid of it, relieved when Maggie hung up and the screen door clicked shut. And who would have called? Someone from her new job, perhaps. Now, with the cat's disappearance summoning forth all the long hours of listening he had done as a child, he remembered the last time he had ever answered the phone. He was just old enough to learn his phone manners and had picked up the receiver while their mother nursed Edwin and their father was out for a walk, for their father was fierce that spring, prowling and pouncing. When Warren said hello, he heard only breathing on the other end of the line, then a strange male voice said, "Guess you know what a naughty man your daddy's been?" Before Warren could formulate the phrase, "May I ask who is calling please?" his grandfather's voice emerged from the darkness of the party line, saying gruffly, "Hello? Who is this?" His grandfather, who never used the phone, had rescued him: the stranger hung up. But then his grandfather had not wanted to talk to Warren. Instead, in a voice barely containing his rage, he said, "Put your father on the line, would you?"

Warren had put the phone down and gone in search of his father, feeling that his grandfather was angry with him for not speaking sharply to the strange man. He had already disappointed his grandfather in other ways, not having quickly taken to fishing or wood carving, too little yet to easily wield the kinds of tools his grandfather valued most. He might have grown into it, might have adapted to the work in spite of himself, but there had been no time—he never spoke to his grandfather again after that day. After their father hung up the phone, pale and trembling, he set back out on foot, the unofficial start to his Wednesday night absences from home. Before he left, however, he found Warren hovering in the dining room, having heard nothing from his father's harsh whispers that made any sense to him. Putting a hand on his son's shoulder with more gentleness than Warren would have thought possible, he said, "Leave the phone calls to me for awhile. If I'm not here, let it ring." And he had. They all had.

* * * *

From his room, Douglas absorbed the squeaking of the kitchen floor below without interest, staring out of his window into the darkness outside. After two nights of having a room to himself he felt as if he were nowhere or in between. He had resented being consigned to the children's room and would not want to return there. His little sisters galled him with their pretence to power and their silly games. Edwin and Quinn had an emerging camaraderie, with Edwin unashamed to cater to Quinn's weakness—the fears, the sadness, the anxiety over everyone getting along. Yet Douglas struggled to fall asleep without the sound of them breathing softly nearby, turning in their bunks, asking him a question on first waking as if he were the only one to know the answer. He had maintained a place amongst the younger ones, whom he dominated and bossed or ignored. But on his own in this room he saw that he was no longer part of the children's world, nor had he joined the ranks of his older siblings. He hadn't been trained to occupy a room alone as Maggie or his brothers had been, moved into single rooms when they were still young.

And so he found that already one desire had replaced another, and that he longed for the impossible: to join his brothers downstairs. His brothers operated on their own terms. After dark it was as if they had the house to themselves, yet they didn't make use of it as they might. At night he never heard their voices gathering in confidence over the dining room table, banishing the domestic spirit of the family dinner and summoning the dark escape of the pub with two bottles of beer, as his father must be doing in the city right now, no matter what was said about Wednesday night meetings. But with a third party, he and his brothers might achieve a spirit of convening, gathering at the living room couch to play cards and share the pipe that Douglas sometimes smoked in his father's shed. Perhaps under these circumstances the theologian would set aside his reading and share with the other two some of what he'd learned—the real ideas that no longer seemed present in his mother's curriculum, which he sensed was quickly coming to an end.

Instead, Douglas was neither a child nor an adult, and in his newly arrived satellite position circling the family, he felt disoriented, easily able to imagine how Maggie could sacrifice her place here. What was here for him? Lately, even reading made him feel removed from reality. Instead of coming back refreshed as he once had, he felt he was clawing to get ashore, where he might then die of thirst. If the book did not immediately consume him, he only read half of it, then set it aside. Doing so, however, made him aware again that he was in the house, and that the house itself seemed to be listening to the story he'd been reading, causing all stories to become their story, the narrative of those who lived in the house. He picked up another book only to experience the same drifting disappointment, the thin predictability that then blurred with the daily monotony of family, a state of inertia without sweat or flesh.

But for a little while he had felt solid today, pushing the mower through the high grass of the back lot. He had worked hard, and felt the triumph and the martyrdom of that work—clipping hedges,

pulling vines, clearing brush. Somewhere in the course of the afternoon, however, he felt the pride of being allowed to skip the trip
to the library and to handle sharp objects give way to the lonely
disorientation of standing in the empty field, feeling the heat on
his shoulders, the sweat running down his chest, the cost of coming
back to life in the aching of his muscles.

Then his mother had come out to greet him, bringing some lem-
onade, a treat possible only by the glass because she would have had to
ask the librarian for a couple packets of sugar. She came to the back
lot with a broad smile, more alert than he had seen her in some time.

"You've done such a beautiful job," she said, gazing at the newly-
shaped meadow, then back toward their proper backyard beyond the
iron gate. She was wearing the white summer sweater and blue wool
skirt that she wore on library days and that would soon—should
already—be too warm for the weather. She rested her hands on her
hips and breathed in the scent of the grass. She rarely strayed beyond
the hedgerow, and so it was unusual to see her brown loafers sinking
into the sharp stalks of newly cut weeds.

He drank from the glass slowly, both to show his appreciation and
because he was unaccustomed to the sweet tartness. As he sipped, he
watched her lift her face toward the sun and then pause, staring at
the house as if she was surprised to learn that this was where they
lived. Her lips remained parted as her eyes swept over the house,
then strayed and caught on some particular detail.

"The girls say there are mulberries," she said, without looking
away from whatever it was that had captured her attention. Her
voice had lost its warmth and grown distant. He recognized this
fluctuation in mood and was angry that his work had failed to buoy

her for longer than a few moments. He did not turn his head to see what she was staring at. She looked at him again, face pale. "Have you ever eaten any?"

He had, he said, but not this year, since it was still too early for them to be properly ripe. She nodded. "I think I'll take a look anyway," she said, and wandered across the meadow toward the tree.

With her back turned, he glanced back at the house to see what she'd seen. In the small window that no one spoke of there was a green glint, as there often was on a good sunny day. Green, blue, and sometimes a flash of yellow came from the window that the children ignored because that was the rule someone had established long ago, accompanied by a punishment that no one could remember or imagine. Yet it had taken his mother less than thirty seconds to, in her own way, undo years of devout inattention, causing the sparkle to seem more like a searchlight. The compliment she'd given him had created its own light, flaring and burning within him, but now it quickly died out.

He might have wanted to join her in picking the berries, hoping for further attention, to rekindle the feeling for which he had just as persistent a need as that emanating from his groin, somewhat abated now in the face of his labors. He did not remember the last time he had talked to his mother without the others around, since Bertie's nap must have allowed her the extravagant pleasure of walking alone to the mulberry tree. Because he saw that it was indeed an extravagant pleasure for her, ducking beneath the tree's lowest branches, and so he did not follow her. Instead, he saw the children disappearing into the cedars, Maggie into the city, his brothers into their rooms, leaving him standing alone in the meadow, afraid. For he was deeply afraid. Someone should pay attention—he had manicured the back lawn.

He decided then to follow his brothers and sisters into the woods. He would scare them, then teach them how to play a good game of war. Leaving his tools, he had circled around the front of the house to approach the cedar stand from the east side. He walked briskly, studying the ground—the beds were eroding here, the bushes needed trimming, a holly tree crowded the front door. Already his vision was being trained. The work of maintenance would demand more and more of his attention; he would have to go inside if he were to get any rest, away from the relentless growing things.

He'd stopped to replace a stone that had fallen away from the border of an old flower bed when he heard a whistle. He looked up, startled. At the other end of the driveway, his old friend Sean stood in a red tee shirt, grinning. Douglas had seen him only at a distance from the library, hanging out with other boys in the parking lot of the high school, and he saw now how much he'd grown.

"Somebody put you to work," Sean said. His hands were shoved into his pockets, as he waited to see how he would be received. At first Douglas saw him as someone who didn't matter. Part of this feeling was born out of injury and rejection, though he understood that their opportunities to play together had been limited by geography, as if there were more than one mile between the town and these sparsely populated acres. A home-schooled kid. A town kid with his own friends. The rest of the feeling was habit: Sean was someone from outside of the inner workings of the family, whose behavior could be observed with detachment, as a diverting story line that only later might suddenly turn on you, threatening to intrude.

Which was ultimately why, of course, Douglas welcomed his old friend with a half-smile, supposing that nothing was at stake for him.

"I was just taking a walk," Sean said casually, careful to say "just," as if to indicate that this was why he had not come seven or eight years ago. "Saw the kids headed into the woods there." He dipped his head in the direction of the cedar stand.

In a moment that felt like the ripping of roots from dry soil, Douglas invited Sean to ambush his siblings in their play by the spider web, which was surely where they would be. They had done so successfully, sneaking up on the four of them where they were planning their next game by the macramé hammock. They were so unaccustomed to the appearance of others and so lost in their play that when he and Sean rushed from the thicket they only stared breathless in silent terror.

In shame at the alarm he had caused them, Douglas felt a flash of rage at Maggie, for whatever it was that she had let out or let in. The anger only intensified moments later when she interrupted their first round of war, and then again when she abandoned them across the swinging bridge. He held onto the anger as they played out their game, letting Sean boss the girls into remaining in the hammock, cajole Quinn into mad runs through the underbrush, and yell at each of them like a soldier would yell, if for no other reason than that none of them would yell back.

Sean had stayed longer than any of them including Douglas expected, since no one called them in for their last lessons, and in their surrender to his leadership they simply waited for him to tell them when the game was over. He did so only after Agnes wandered away from the hammock a time or two, mumbling about boredom with surprisingly plaintive submission. When Sean finally left, he did so with a shrug and a wave, exhibiting an easy withdrawal from a couple hours of play. Douglas, on the other hand, felt as if he really had endured a war, just as he also felt that he needed his friend to return as much as he'd needed Maggie's room. They would retreat there next time, away from his younger siblings, for some more peaceable form of play.

And yet now, lying in bed after a hard day's work, Douglas longed only for his father's return, his late night tread on the stairs. As he drifted toward unconsciousness, exhausted by his rotating desires, Douglas thought that he heard the faint cry of a cat. For a moment, his eyes flickered open. Before he was swallowed by the darkness of sleep, he saw a small circle of yellow light flash from the cane brake like a group of synchronized fireflies.

CHAPTER TEN

Maggie had no idea how she had come to be in this place. Leaving her grandmother's house, she was fairly confident that just a few more paces through the stand of cedars would bring her to the cornfield, the barn perched against the hill to guide her home. And yet each step forward only brought her deeper into the woods as the cedars gave way to locust trees and to more undergrowth—to bushes with thorns, to fallen logs and grape vines blocking her path, all only faintly lit by the moonlight. Maggie considered turning back, but her conviction that she was following an internal compass toward home was hard to shake, as was the conviction that, should she find her way back to her grandparents, no answer would come to a knock on the front door. Perhaps she'd always plunged forward without much regard for what lay scattered behind, so little of which could be considered a loss, the forgotten neighbors and kin too busy tending their own wounds.

When she came upon a narrow creek—the same, she hoped, that wound through the cane brake by the fat lady's house—she stayed as near as she could to the bed, following the water's dim reflection. After a while the creek, which had been seeping along noiselessly, began to patter as though falling against a tin roof. Stopping to get her bearings, Maggie gazed ahead to where the banks rose above the surface of the water, a few feet on each side. There, a round metal culvert had been buried into the creek bed, with water running through the dark shadows beneath the flat surface of a trail. She squatted, her arms wrapped around her knees, and listened for sounds from the drain, conscious of her grandmother's warnings about tramps. She had crouched in just this manner on some other day long ago, the creek having been frozen solid. In a rare mischievous moment that she only now recalled, she had sneaked away from the house to lie in wait for her father, out roaming the grounds checking the fences, though there was nothing to keep in, nothing to keep out. Had he passed above, she intended to jump out from beneath the culvert like the troll and demand that he give her the secret password before crossing, something she felt he would indulge. There had been that time, a brief interval when he hummed softly while tying knots.

But he had not come, and in waiting, Maggie only heard a piercing shriek that she took to be the mountain lion, who was said to have once lured men into the woods by sounding like a woman in need of rescue. She remained still, heart racing, until the cougar shrieking became her mother screaming for her to come home, the only time in childhood that Maggie heard any voice raised. She assumed the shrieking noise had been her mother all along, calling until Maggie arrived breathless at the back gate. In a rare moment of undress, her mother stood at the backdoor in an unbuttoned wool housedress with Quinn on her hip and one breast exposed. "It's too dangerous," she said to Maggie, scanning the property behind her as if she too expected a starving beast to come bounding from the forest. "You'll catch your death of cold in this snow."

Now, hearing nothing, Maggie climbed the bank above the culvert to see where the road might lead. There, a wide gravel trail split in three directions, forming a T where she stood. One branch seemed to go back the way she'd come, toward her grandparents' house, winding through the woods away from the creek. The other disappeared into the woods on the far side of the creek, perhaps leading back toward the cornfields, though the trees were thick and she could not be sure. The third, which she took now, ran alongside the creek in the direction she'd been pursuing. The trees became tall poplars, and the underbrush thinned on each side of the path. Making her way here was easier.

In a few moments, a small stone house appeared on the left, lit from inside. It teetered on a slope, the front yard dipping before rising again to meet the trail, forming a flood zone with puddles and smears of red clay. Across the grassy space a couple of boards lay as a bridge for crossing. A vagrant would live here above any other place that Maggie could imagine. After a moment's hesitation, she tread past the house as quietly as possible, hoping to reach the woods on the other side of the clearing without incurring notice.

She had just passed the plank when the front door to the house creaked open. Maggie did not slow down or speed up, but kept walking, staring straight ahead.

"I wouldn't mind having a better look at you," an old woman's voice called, "since you're here."

Maggie stopped, recognizing the voice immediately. She turned to see a short, lumpy silhouette clutching the door knob. "Who are you?" Maggie asked, somewhat alarmed. She was tired of adapting, of responding to the terms established by others. She could have asked this question any number of times in the last three days: of the fat lady, the receptionist, the witch, the neighbor boy, or her grandparents. She could have put the question to her father for leaving her in the coffee shop, to her mother for sleeping late oblivious to her rat bite, or to Phillip for all but warning her against a walk in the woods. Who were any of these people, and how had she come to be among them?

The woman gave a wracking cough before she replied. "I always did like your brothers better than you," she said. "Now I remember why."

But Maggie did not need her grandmother to identify herself, as perhaps her grandmother had already guessed, leaving the front door open but disappearing inside the house. Maggie tested the thin boards, and when they seemed sturdy, crossed the muddy yard. Once on the other side, she stepped from the boards to a cinder-block and through the doorway. In the living room to the left, her grandmother sat on a couch watching the television that was pushed into the corner. She had a cigarette propped in one hand, the smoke curling in the lamp light. She was wearing blue pants, tennis shoes that were unaccountably white in these backwoods, and a yellow tee shirt. After a moment, she tipped her cigarette into an ashtray on a coffee table that was covered with magazines and newspapers, the brown wrinkled skin hanging from her arm. Maggie could not help but stare at her, this woman who seemed conjured from imagination rather than memory.

"Pick a couch," her grandmother said, nodding with a head full of tight gray curls. Maggie shut the door behind her and stepped into the room, sitting across from her grandmother on one of two couches that formed an L shape, the fabric a rough mute floral not dissimilar from their couch at home.

"In this show," her grandmother pointed to the television with the cigarette, "they never can quite get it together." She sat across from Maggie, watching steadily. "They're always trying to get it together, but then they don't." Suddenly she erupted into laughter that quickly devolved into a series of coughs. Maggie turned her attention to the screen, on which a group of people were talking in a living room.

"I could get you a beer," her grandmother said without looking over at her. Apparently her grandmother had wanted a look at her that didn't require actual looking. Maggie had grown up, but her grandmother would not comment on this as if it were an achievement—everyone grew up. "Nonalcoholic beer. That's all I drink." She gestured to the kitchen, a dark room on the other side of an open doorway. "It tastes like shit, but then, you don't get addicted."

"No, thank you," Maggie said. She scanned the room for something to ask about, a place to start. She had been mostly compliant these last three days, meeting strangers with their implicit and explicit demands. And she'd been mostly compliant for a lifetime before that. Here she would be direct. Find out why her grandmother had abandoned her.

On the wall, she saw a wooden plaque that read, "Someday I'm going to have a nervous breakdown – I've worked for it, I've earned it, and no one is going to deprive me of it!" Beside the plaque was a poster with a picture of a rag doll being put through a laundry wringer, her cloth face grimacing and the wringer caught around her waist. The poster said, "The truth will set you free. But first it will make you miserable." As neither of these items invited polite query, Maggie finally pointed to a side table cluttered with a group of gold trophies. "What are your trophies for?" she asked.

"Bowling," her grandmother said. "You can see that by the figure bowling on the top." She did not seem to be sarcastic. Maggie squinted and saw that indeed, the small women on the top were holding bowling balls. "I am a bowler. Or I was."

"I've never been bowling," Maggie said. On the television the family was fighting playfully. Someone groaned and someone else giggled.

"No. You wouldn't have." Her grandmother waited for the punch line to be delivered on the show, then pointed to a newspaper on the table. "I just read this today. Can you believe it? It says that someone spotted Bigfoot recently. A big hairy man-giant thing, up north someplace."

Maggie looked at the front cover, which pictured a furry man just disappearing behind a pine tree. "Bigfoot?" Maggie echoed, disoriented. She was beginning to feel hungry again, and she found she had an unaccountable desire to hold Lula, whom she hoped had been fed by someone else in the family. She understood that no one would be waiting up for her when she finally returned, and that no one would ask her where she'd been. What would her father do when he arrived home to find her bench empty?

"I get the papers from a gas station just off the highway," her grandmother said. "Every day but Friday there's a new one. I used to ride there on the back of your grandfather's motorcycle when we lived in town, but now I walk. It's a little ways but there's nothing else to do. Each day there's something incredible in these papers. There's a word your mom would use. Incredible. I don't really believe any of it myself. How did they get this picture of Bigfoot, for starters? Were they just hanging out waiting on him? They could have been doing something else, I guess. They could have been deer hunting, for example. Not the newspaper people, of course, but the people who gave the picture to the newspaper. And they got paid, maybe? Would they have gotten paid for this picture?" She glanced at Maggie, and when Maggie did not answer, looked back toward the television.

"But even if you don't believe the stories, and I don't believe them, not any of them, they're all worth thinking about. Somebody made this stuff up. And so it's possible. It's all possible—the monsters or aliens or ghosts or whatever. And so in a way I do believe in the stories after all. But unlike this newspaper," she pointed to the thin tabloid, "I don't really think that anything should be done about any of it. I don't think that there's much of a disaster if Bigfoot is walking around the frozen plains or forests or tundra, whatever it's like where he's at. But then I don't live there, and so he doesn't scare me. Maybe it'd be different, closer to home. Take your family, for instance. Maybe you'd want to decide which member of your family might be an alien or a unicorn or a witch or any other so-called mythical creature—a centaur, that's another one—and then you'd want to decide what needed to be done about that, if anything. And of course in your family, you've got lots to choose from." Her grandmother leaned back against the couch and propped one foot up on the coffee table.

Maggie said nothing, overwhelmed by the monologue, which unlike the receptionist's talk, intimidated rather than seduced. She picked up another one of the tabloids, thinking of her family members. "I don't suppose any of us is really a centaur," she said, aware that she was speaking a little too literally.

"You don't suppose," her grandmother said flatly.

Maggie scanned the first story in the newspaper, looking for ways to participate in this conversation that her grandmother might appreciate. She suddenly wanted to show gratitude: this was the woman who had once handed her a bowl of freshly whipped cream mixed with sugar and vanilla to eat beneath the dining room table, telling her father to go to hell when he protested that it would make his daughter sick, which it had not. "I don't think it's true that this woman gave birth to a child who was half-pig," Maggie said, belatedly picking up her grandmother's subject. She flipped to another story about an invasion of insects. "I don't think any of these are true at all."

"Unlike the things you read," her grandmother replied, eyeing Maggie's knapsack as if she knew it contained a book.

Maggie opened her mouth to protest, then remembered she was currently reading a story about talking rabbits. She thought about explaining the differences in the types of stories to her grandmother, but she couldn't quite think of how best to do so, any more than she had once been able to tell her other grandmother of the poisonous impact of her daily television show. Before she could try, her grandmother had opened a drawer in the coffee table from which she pulled a clear jar filled with liquid. She slid the container over to Maggie.

"Here's a true thing—a curiosity—something you loved when you were a child," she chuckled. Maggie picked up the jar. Floating in the clear liquid was two inches of pale flesh. Maggie nearly dropped the glass container.

Her grandmother laughed again. "That's half your grandfather's pointer finger," she said. Maggie set the jar back down on the coffee table, trembling just a little. "The half that got hacked off by the engine of a lawnmower that he was trying to fix. The rest of him's buried in town and so isn't it interesting that this little piece is probably better kept than that which is in that shiny expensive box?" She'd half-turned toward Maggie now, her watery blue eyes bloodshot. She lit a new cigarette and waved the smoke from her face as if it was someone else's and bothering her. "Of course, he's not one to be treasured, since thirty years ago this month he was sleeping with the neighbor's wife." She grunted. "Affairs, if one is to have one, really shouldn't be conducted with the neighbor's wife, who lies out in the sun tanning. Wouldn't you agree?" She looked at Maggie directly. "It's a bit beyond common decency, and there's common decency, even when it comes to affairs. But you might not know this. Do you have a boyfriend yet?"

Maggie merely shook her head, unable to keep up with her grandmother's train of thought.

"Well, you will."

"I don't want a boyfriend," Maggie said, not really expecting to be taken seriously.

Her grandmother looked sharply at her. "You like girls?" she said.

Maggie was confused. "I'm sorry?"

Her grandmother shrugged. "I thought perhaps it ran in the family."

"I don't want children," Maggie said, even though she knew she could not explain herself to her grandmother, who would only assume that her own forecasts for the future were right, as did all adults.

"Ah, now there's a subject we can agree on. Children make you fat, and then they need things from you, an awful lot of things you can't always give them, partly because you don't know what exactly it is they're wanting, and partly because giving them the things that they're wanting can leave you with nothing. You've really got to hold onto a certain number of things or else you've got nothing, are nothing, are treated like nothing, even by the children who took the things from you."

"My mother wanted children," Maggie said, feeling, as a child of sorts herself, that children needed defending somehow.

"Didn't she, though. How many of you are there now?"

"Nine."

Her grandmother nodded, staring at the television again. "A sea of children to love and be loved by."

"I'm going to the city to work at a church nursery," Maggie said.

"That's a funny thing to do for someone who doesn't want kids."

"It's the only thing I know how to do," Maggie said.

"It's the only thing most women know how to do, or think they know, and so do badly, usually, until they learn how to do something else. In your case, I'd say the sooner the better. In the meantime, if you make yourself too available around here, as wandering around the woods at night surely indicates you must be doing, someone else will pick you out to do their own kind of work."

"What did you do?" Maggie asked, remembering her intention to ask questions.

Her grandmother thought for a moment. "I worked in a shoe factory for a while," she said. She held up one neat white tennis shoe. "They do so much better with shoes these days. These cost seven dollars. If I don't go outside in them, I can keep them clean."

"They're nice," Maggie said politely.

"Yes, and so cheap, someone must have bled for them." She paused. "And then I kept house. I ironed. I ironed a lot. I could wring a chicken neck well enough. And I could bowl. I also watched out the window for when the neighbor lady came out to tan and I cursed her. Usually from the window and maybe a time or two from the yard itself, I cursed her. I got driven to the hospital to be electrocuted, because that's what they did for women who cursed other people, believing themselves to actually have some power for harm. They gave you valium for your nerves, diet pills for your weight, then when you got too attached to the valium or the diet pills they drove you to the hospital to jolt it all out of your system—a fresh start." She took a drag from her cigarette. "And then of course somewhere in there I accidentally raised your mother to be a mother of her own."

"But not any others?" Maggie said.

Her grandmother looked sharply at her. "What others?" she snapped.

"Weren't there ever any other babies?" Maggie wondered just how angry her grandmother could become. She might swoop down on her as she had once done to snatch the stethoscope, saying, *These are not toys, you brat.*

"Who told you about that?" her grandmother said.

Maggie remained quiet. No one had told her. Not her mother, certainly.

"Could be I told you, I guess," her grandmother said, shrugging, "when your mama brought you along to care for me when I was in a bad way. More than once she's told me I've got a knack for the inappropriate. Which was no doubt why she stopped coming around at all. To protect her children from my spoiling influence, I believe she said." She paused, as if considering the degree to which her behavior at that time might have impacted the children.

"But your mother more than made up for my losses in the baby department. She outdid herself. Under the circumstances, I might have thought that there would be a limit. I did think that there would be a limit, but she had her own ideas about things. For all the good it's done her."

Maggie was not sure what to say to this. In some ways, her grandmother was disclosing more than all the rest, and in other ways, she was just as cryptic as the others had been. Feeling a wave of hunger, she remembered the chocolate peanut butter balls that her other grandmother had given her and pulled them from her backpack.

"Would you like a sweet?" she said, holding out the paper bag.

Her grandmother peered inside, then reached in and pulled out a candy. "I can't believe that your parents let you eat these," she said, biting into one. She didn't ask how Maggie had come by the treat, but closed her eyes, savoring the taste before she popped the other half of the chocolate ball into her mouth. "It's good, isn't it?" she said with her mouth full.

Maggie bit into one as well. The chocolate gave and then the peanut butter crumbled against her tongue. This was better, even, than the cupcake, pudding, or sweet hot tea. "Mhmm," she said. She coughed with the force of the sweetness, then took another bite. "I've never had one of these before."

"Well then you should know that it will never taste quite as good as it does right now," her grandmother said, reaching into the bag for another. "Take it from a natural optimist. I'm not surprised you've never had one before now, but I'd be surprised if you didn't have another before long, once you're in the city. Careful you don't become addicted."

"Is that why our parents don't allow sweets?" Maggie said.

Her grandmother shrugged. "Your parents had their own ideas about how to raise you, as all parents do, and of course they wanted you healthy, without illness. And maybe they also didn't want you to end up like me, or like my neighbor down the way, big as a house."

"The fat lady?" Maggie asked with her mouth full of candy. She was relieved: she had been getting her bearings after all, and could soon be home.

"Fat lady?" her grandmother said scornfully, as if she herself had not just called her neighbor big as a house. "If you mean Mamie, then yes, that's her." She squinted at Maggie a moment, as if she were finally getting that good look at her after all. "Your mother certainly didn't go out of her way to teach you any manners."

Maggie flushed, knowing that the good moment between them had passed. She should leave now. "I want to be sure of my way home," she said, pushing the empty paper bag back into her knapsack. "This path leads past the cane brake and on up the hill?"

Her grandmother nodded, turning back toward the television now, ignoring Maggie as she stood. Maggie stepped toward the door, then hesitated. "Can you please tell me—should I be worried about tramps?"

Her grandmother chuckled, staring at the television. "There's more than one kind of tramp," she said. "I suspect you've already seen what there is to see."

When the front door shut behind her a moment later, Maggie breathed deeply, aware that she'd been exposed in her ignorance in a manner that she did not fully comprehend. She hadn't thanked her grandmother for the visit nor had she been invited back, and so she felt that just as soon as she had ventured into this new territory she could not return. And yet, though she did not intend to come back, she understood that once you've ventured into a new place, you'll end up there again and again whether you want to or not. She had been ambling about carelessly, biding her time and avoiding her own house as if that was where the worst danger lay. If she wasn't careful, she wouldn't be at the proper place at the proper time in order to leave for the city with her father on Friday morning.

Not long after Maggie crossed the footbridge and returned to the path, she saw the woods open up at the back corner of the fat lady—of Mamie's—house. The yard was partially illuminated by light from the basement windows covered in white curtains. Perhaps Mamie was baking even now. In the backyard, a picnic table was nearly buried in the high weeds a few feet from the back door to the house, the one that lead to the original kitchen. The rotting table reminded Maggie of her arrival to a Halloween party here many years ago, pushed in the wheel barrel and wearing the mermaid costume. All the children from the neighborhood and from town had come for treats—for caramel apples, spider cupcakes, and chocolate marshmallows melted over the bonfire. The grass had been mowed, and from the trees Mamie had strung white lights that glowed through paper pumpkin faces. Warren and Phillip must have been there, though she did not remember them. Perhaps she and her brothers had met the receptionist's boys in the woods behind their own backyard, as her brothers would have been too little to push Maggie down the hill themselves.

They gathered at the table, and Mamie served them spiced cider, as the night was cool. Her daughter was dressed like a stained-glass window, with a cardboard frame hanging from her shoulders.

Behind the frame a colored tissue-paper design was taped to a sheet of plastic and lit with a small flashlight dangling from around her neck. Mamie's husband was dressed like a hobo with an unshaven face, wearing suspenders and rolled up pants and bare feet, with a bandana tied to the end of a cane pole. He spent the evening pretending he'd just hopped off the train and that in his wanderings through the woods, had stumbled upon this party. He pretended this very seriously, occasionally limping up to his daughter to deliver compliments to the host. Maggie felt he might really leave and not return, as truly he had eventually done.

After everyone had eaten, they circled the fire and Mamie began telling ghost stories, threatening to sit on the children if they did not listen, or to banish them to the empty stone house that sat deep in the woods, where Maggie's grandmother now lived. Mamie did not need to threaten, however, as she told her tales well, the children forgetting their last drops of cider as they listened to a story from the old days about a woman buried alive after a long illness. Still in a coma, they had buried her, Maggie remembered, thinking her dead. Yet in the middle of the night after the funeral, the husband and children awakened to the sound of the mother's voice at the front door, begging to be let in. Thinking they were haunted by her ghost, they refused, until the eldest daughter, the smartest one, looked out the window toward the barn to see whether their mother's trusted horse recognized her, hanging his head from his stall and whinnying a greeting as was his custom. Sure enough, the horse did not shy from the ghost, but knew its owner. The family opened the door, welcoming their weak and weary mother, who was smeared with mud and full of story: a grave robber had come to steal her wedding ring, and when he could not pry it past the swollen joint, tried to cut off her finger. The mother awoke to the searing pain of the deep gash and to the sight of the grave robber, hopping from the grave and running away into the night. She had dragged herself all the way home from the cemetery.

Hadn't the story ended happily? The mother regained her health and lived among her family once again. But everyone listening around the fire shivered at the ending that they themselves could imagine, being raised by a mother who had returned from horror with the smell of damp soil in her skirts. The ride home by wheelbarrow would be long that night and the snow would soon come and Maggie would think that it might have been better for the mother not to come back at all, so the rest of them could trust death's finality.

As she turned from the house toward home, the dry breeze that Maggie had felt earlier tossed the heads of cane above her. And yet even amid the rustle of leaves, she could hear a still more distinct movement from the base of the stalks, a noise that did not fit the pattern of the other noises, that was out of step with the whole. Turning toward the crunch in the undergrowth, she thought she saw a small flicker of light deep amid the cane. She watched, barely breathing, but the light was gone.

Afraid, Maggie ran all the way past the cane brake, past the woodpile with broken glass and across the creek. She climbed over the fence and resumed running up the hill, a stitch in her side. When she reached the iron archway she was out of breath and could run no farther. She stopped and looked up: in the round window on the second floor of the house, a pale yellow light glowed.

CHAPTER ELEVEN

Martin didn't know how long he had been standing in the mud, staring at the house, when he saw his daughter cross the far side of Mamie's yard. He quickly stepped farther back into the reeds and turned off the flashlight. Maggie paused, peered at the cane brake, then broke into a run. Only after she remained gone for some time did he let out a sigh of relief. He'd only just missed an uncomfortable encounter, one he would not have been able to explain. What Maggie was doing here he could not guess, only that she had been traveling the path that led from her grandmother's house. His mother-in-law was capricious, capable of revealing so much. In what way had she tainted this spring evening for her granddaughter?

Just as Martin felt sure that Maggie would not return and was about to push his way through the reeds, the basement door opened, throwing a patch of light onto the ground. A silhouette climbed the flight of stairs up to the yard—long smooth nose, heavy jaw, bulky body. In the second between the door opening and the man appearing, Martin's blood surged forward irrationally, some portion of his brain expecting a tall, thin form to step onto the turf, lean against his cane, and wave an oversized flashlight above his head in an arc. Having walked all the way from the gravel road in a fit of nostalgia,

Martin could easily imagine he was watching a handsome man in his mid-thirties wait for a flicker of light from the round window on the hill. Once the signal had come all those years ago—and it would have come quickly, unmistakably, as a matter of some routine— Jeremy would have begun walking toward the cottage where Martin's mother-in-law now lived, to all appearances simply taking a break from soldering together bits of colored glass into lamps and windows.

The shadow now standing before him lit a pipe. Mamie had taken a companion, some type of poor substitute who, even though he appeared to have full use of all his limbs, had taken no better care of the property than her ex-husband. Martin breathed shallowly and remained motionless, feeling a surge of hatred for her, still so unable to be more discerning. Jeremy always said there were never any entirely unnoticed exits, not for anyone. Instead, the two of them had relied upon a thin layer of deception—insomnia and late-night artistic inspiration and walks for the stiff hip—something that was needed but that barely kept off the chill. And yet later Mamie would still play victim, insisting on utter betrayal as if she had been swathed tightly and thickly in warmth all along.

She was too smart to be as betrayed as she had affected to be all those years ago, coming home early from what was supposed to be a week-long visit with her parents an hour or so away, having taken their daughter and left her husband to his work. Her absence from home granted a rare opportunity further blessed by the unexpected snowstorm that caused Martin's heart to leap upon waking—he could not go to work. He had time ahead of him. He had mounds of shoveling ahead of him. He trembled his way through breakfast, and as soon as he could, pulled on a layer of long underwear beneath an old mechanic's jumpsuit belonging to his father-in-law, then thick wool socks and tall wading boots, the warmest he owned since they did not get such deep snow very often. As he worked he anticipated his and Jeremy's break from feeding the wood stove in the chilly cottage, from the risky spiral of smoke that anyone observant enough could notice, particularly his father, who owned the old hunting outpost. Instead they could stay warm at Jeremy's house in afternoon visits that Martin would create by checking fence posts and monitoring the property line, chores his father said he never did enough of because of his cushy job with bureaucrats in the city. Martin would be able to watch Jeremy work, as he'd only done once before, when they first met at a small street festival in town and discovered they were neighbors. They might have carpet beneath them for a change, or a real bed.

These thoughts carried him while he shoveled the driveway and ate lunch, on until early afternoon when, having taken the long way to Jeremy's house, he was delighted to find that the river cane was entirely bowed under the weight of the snow. The cane created a solid arc from one side of the creek to the other with a dark tunnel below where the water trickled. Martin felt like a child, joyous, wanting to surprise someone, trick someone, risk absurdity. So without letting Jeremy know he was there, he climbed the cane. He was pleased by just how easy it was, sturdy branches giving him foothold. He kept expecting Jeremy to ascend from the basement to shout a greeting at him—to luxuriate in the shouting of the greeting—and so he hurried, wanting to hail him first from the top of the arc of cane, which did not give beneath him. Once there, he turned toward his lover's house and then leaned back, gloved hands grasping the reeds beneath him, then letting go: he was suspended. He listened to the gurgle of the creek, feeling both the warmth from his exertions and the cold air around him, the freezing and steaming of his skin. At this angle, no part of him could be seen from the house he had left behind, full of studying children, wary of his unusual good mood.

And so in the pure excitement of what he hoped would be the three, maybe even four days given to them by this snow, he unzipped his pants and took the hard cock bulging there since waking and pulled it through the opening in the jumpsuit and the long underwear and his boxers, the balls and base buried warmly so that what remained was shorter than it should have been but still boldly signaling to the man inside. He placed his hands behind his head and called his lover's name once or twice before he heard laughter from the bedroom window, at which time he shifted his hips in an attempt to wiggle his penis in the air—a flag of surrender that he was only in this moment able to own up to, to give in to as soon as he descended to find Jeremy waiting in boots and robe, wrapped in a wool blanket. They were only there for a few moments, but those moments, and what they said in them, and the cold that began to reach them as soon as those moments had passed, caused them to forget the blanket on the railing of the back porch as they went inside, the semen crusting over the surface like a fine frost.

Which might not have mattered at all, had Mamie not returned early, as early as the slowly melting snow would allow, to find Martin quietly crocheting while Jeremy cut a new pattern for a window, by all accounts a happy domestic scene in the snug basement. Martin politely apologized for smoking indoors and affected as much masculinity as he could with a ball of russet yarn unraveling at his feet, the previous two days having undone years of polished performance. They were simply neighbors fighting off cabin fever together, his behavior said, as he pulled on his boots and made a joke about needing a break from the chaos of his children. Yet even before he passed the empty hunting cottage on the long route home, Mamie's screams from the back porch echoed eerily in the hushed winter landscape. He would later learn that she had dumped the blanket in the river cane and broken all of Jeremy's stained glass over the top of the woodpile. The next morning, she delivered a cake to Martin's parents with the message, "Your son is a fag," inscribed on the top in pink icing. His wife she left to her own devices, as if in punishment for her willful ignorance.

Now Mamie's companion finally finished his pipe and retreated, closing the door behind him. Martin waited until the basement went black, then emerged from his hiding place. He took the path to his mother-in-law's cottage, the ground rising beneath him and the reeds giving way to blackberry bushes and a grove of redbud trees. Before he entered the woods, he stopped and turned to look back at his own house. He expected to see the landing lit up by Maggie, reading before bed. Instead, the landing was dark, and the one light that was shining on the second floor came from the round window. For a moment, it was as if Martin had become Jeremy, delighted his signal had been seen—his lover was on the way. Then with a sinking feeling he knew that for the first time since their move into the house, someone was in his room. And though Maggie had certainly ventured into more places than he imagined she was capable of since their trip to the city two days ago, he doubted that the person sitting in the old servant quarters right now could be anyone but his wife. He ducked his head and entered the woods.

At the crude footbridge leading to the hunting cottage, Martin hesitated, listening to the peeper frogs and wondering what would happen when he arrived home tonight. After a moment, Annette opened the front door and stood there without speaking. He walked heavily across the planks, unsure whether he had energy for this obligatory visit. Annette would have seen him pass earlier, cutting across her property from his parking place along the back road. She would expect him to stop in. Besides, he was curious about what she might have said to Maggie. Not that it mattered now, with Hannah sifting through whatever things he'd left behind in the concealed room.

By the time he reached the doorway, Annette had returned to the couch and was smoking. She pushed a newspaper onto the floor to give him room to sit beside her.

"You've come during my favorite," she said, pointing to the television with her cigarette. "It's just started." She would not make herself immediately available to him just because he'd indulged a fit of nostalgia, she was saying, and so he settled into his end of the couch to patiently await whatever attention she wanted to bestow. But of course he could not help but remember the stack of pillows and blankets that had once been tucked into the unfinished attic in case his father should check on the old place during his rounds of the property. When he and Jeremy were using the cottage, Martin possessed the astonishing ability to believe he was free from the peering scrutiny of in-laws and parents, the silent pleading of wife and children, the sleeping suspicions of his own employees at work, all apparently oblivious to his transformation, to this act of becoming someone he had always and yet never been.

And hadn't those moments of freedom been real, in spite of everything to follow? Because what came next had left him disoriented—his parents no longer speaking to him, his wife in apparent ignorance but having abandoned all expectations, his neighbors never clearly allies or enemies. He sometimes wished Hannah had let him go the way that Mamie had her husband, turning Jeremy out of house and town and threatening to reveal a truth everyone had somehow come to know anyhow; soon people stopped buying her cakes, as if her husband's affliction might taint the air she baked in. But then, Martin could also picture all too well what that new world of freedom would have been for him: a faraway place that allowed him and Jeremy to live together as family, but with unfamiliar work and landscape and routines, and without his own family to buoy, bully, or sustain. Unlike Jeremy, who had come a stranger to this town with family in tow, Martin was too firmly rooted in these mountains, having only ever gone from family to family, the natural course of events. But that was when his wife's ignorance had allowed him a choice. Now he could not be so sure.

Martin rose to get a drink of water, unsettled. In the kitchen, he retrieved a glass and reached out of habit for one of the packaged cookies Annette kept in a bowl on the counter. He ate the iced oatmeal while staring into the shadows outside the window, letting the crumbs fall into the sink. When he first told his mother-in-law about this neglected property, her husband had only just passed away. Martin had not seen her in years and had not spoken to his own parents except to get permission from his father for Annette to use the house. His in-laws had been living in a house they rented in town, the one that Mamie's daughter stayed in now, but the rent would be difficult for Annette to manage on her own. In Martin's last memory of his father-in-law, the old man was standing on the front porch with a rifle aimed at Martin, who had one hand on the fence latch, keeping up the Sunday visits that his wife had abandoned some time before. He hadn't needed his father-in-law to speak to know what had happened; he'd only been taken aback that someone had known and that someone had told, someone who was not his wife. It could have been anyone.

In his last visit to his mother-in-law's before her husband's death he found her ironing sheets at two o'clock in the morning, the amphetamine from her diet pills keeping her up all night. He'd gone for her because his wife was birthing their eighth child, and though the midwife was on her way, he hoped this might be a moment when mother and daughter could reconcile, Annette helping for the next few days, taking some of the work off of Maggie's small shoulders. Annette had never much cared for children, but in her moments of clarity she could be efficient and practical. When he arrived, however, he saw that she would be incapable of assisting anyone. He did not even mention that Hannah was in labor, or that he had just dropped six of the children at his mother's for the night. Instead, he created some excuse for why he was driving through town in the middle of the night and happened to see her light on. She barely seemed to need explanations, as she pressed the iron against the white sheets and spoke harshly and at length about her neighbors' faults while her husband slept on in their bedroom. As she talked and ironed without any regard for Martin, he felt a strange affinity for the suffering coursing through the erratic movements of her plump body—she sent the iron over the sheet too quickly, tipping it against the thick corners of the hem, and yet she was an expert, in command. He felt paralyzed—he needed to get back home. Finally he roused his father-in-law to make sure she did not burn down the house and left.

Back in the living room at home, the midwife had arrived and his wife's body was bent to the task of bringing life into a family that even with so many children had been silent for so long that he could not remember the source of inspiration that lead to this child. Some silent entreaty on her part, an efficient response on his. As only children themselves, they had always wanted a small brood, but he had been outmatched by her insatiable need. In the living room, his wife shouted at him for bothering at all with her worthless mother, and he could not explain how his mother-in-law's pain had for a few moments somehow taken priority over hers, over Maggie's, standing silently against the wood stove as if politely waiting to be excused. Later, he also could not explain to his wife why her mother's pain should command some compassion, some forgiveness. Her inability to help with the birth of this child should not be held against her. But Hannah would not have her children uncertain about the scope of their grandmother's love the way she had been as a child, she said. She would lose herself in the world of her children, without need for her mother or his, nor for the town neighbors whose witness of her parents' daily fighting made her share in their shame, nor for the military divorcee with her aggressive and untrustworthy sons, nor for—and here his heart lurched—the effete artist and his eccentric wife. Here her complaints, so rarely aired with such intensity, stopped altogether. Still, he wanted to tell her how for those brief moments she had sounded exactly like her mother and that he'd been afraid for her, afraid for his part in making her so.

On the television, a commercial began to blare now. Annette turned to speak as he returned from the kitchen. "Your daughter was here tonight," she said.

He didn't reply, taking a seat on the couch. She spoke as if he had only one. For her this was essentially true.

"Said her work here was done. Said she was off to the city to take care of other people's children. I told her, I said, 'Maggie, that's wonderful now honey, it really is, and I wish the best for you.'" She chuckled. "I said, 'the city, well, they say that's the place to chase your dreams.'"

"Did you now."

"Well, she needed some encouragement. Said she was a little scared. That's all, she said, only a little."

Martin waited for Annette to finish with the preliminaries in which she fabricated details, telling an embellished version of a conversation, trying to make whatever point it was that she wanted to make—that he had limited the opportunities for his children, that he had squelched their emotional range. "Probably not a side of her you see much, the scared side. Probably not something she shows to y'all all that often." She turned toward the television as the show came back on.

"She'll do all right there," he said. He pictured the stone interior walls of the church where he had dropped Maggie off on Monday—the efficient click of the director's heels as she led Maggie from the lobby, the paunchy doorman who let him out. Maggie had as much as asked for a nunnery, and that was more or less what she would get. What choices were there but variations on four sturdy walls and people inside those walls with whom to share meals and people outside those walls to regard warily? Maggie would be dry and fed, she'd still get to take long walks and read. She'd be with other people, which Annette, alone most days in this shack, could scarcely criticize.

"She'd been to your parents'," Annette said without taking her eyes from the screen, as if she were reading a crystal ball. Martin imagined that she could see Maggie as she settled onto her bench to try to sleep, wondering why her mother was crying from a part of the house she'd never seen before, waiting for the sound of her father's car on the gravel, not knowing whether his arrival would make things better or worse. Worse, he could tell her, so much worse that he would leave them all alone for now. Each decade of his life had become a separate dream, compact and sustained for a time until one self died and was replaced by another. In the hidden room his wife was now waking from her dream, and the person that emerged would not recognize his place among them, would not accommodate a stranger. He would sneak in to get some things, and then he would go. He glanced down the hallway toward the empty spare bedroom of the cottage. Where else?

"She didn't say anything about it, of course," Annette said. "No surprises there. But she'd stopped off and had herself a visit."

"You think so?" Martin said. He didn't know whether his mother-in-law was telling the truth. He'd once tried to explain to her that she created mistrust with her exaggerations, but she had snorted and then broken into peals of laughter. Say that again, she said. That part about mistrust, I'd like to hear it again. "Everything I say is true," she said, "and what's true is that my daughter married a man with no—," here she paused as if choosing from an abundance of traits that he lacked, "—no sense of humor." She wanted him to know she really meant to say something else, something crude, but was choosing to spare him. "I'll shoot your cock off," his father-in-law had finally yelled after Martin turned away from their fence. He was aware that in the eyes of his in-laws, and in the eyes of all of those on the street who had heard his father yell, he was a man both with and without a cock. They would have it their way: he was a predator and a pussy, someone to be feared and scorned. At that moment, he'd have shoved it into anyone who needed help sorting out the difference.

Annette was waiting, wanting him to express more interest in her news. "How do you know she'd been to visit them?" he finally said.

"I know she was at your mother's," Annette scowled at him, "because she had some of her peanut butter balls. She shared them with me."

Martin could almost taste the achingly sweet treat of childhood, something with which the packaged cookies that Annette kept could not compare. "Maggie's had a full night, then," he said without inflection. None of it mattered now, what Maggie saw or knew, or who told her what, not with his wife sitting in the hidden room. Still, his parents. He'd not seen them in so long.

"I'd say she's had a full night all right," Annette said as the show resumed. She was proud of her own contribution, the satisfying shock of her existence in this mud hole that Maggie had taken bewildered but in stride. Though Annette was happy enough to have two visitors in one evening, they were each so preoccupied with their own thoughts that her house was like a shabby harbor where one would resupply only in the worst of conditions. A while back, Martin had suggested that because he did not visit very often, coming only occasionally to bring her the heavier food and cleaning supplies, they should do something else instead of watching television, which she could do anytime alone. Hadn't they always liked gin rummy when the children were younger? He spoke as if he was not sure, but nevertheless looked around the scant furnishings of the cottage as if for a pack of cards.

To oblige him, she'd turned the television down low and pulled a deck from the drawer in the coffee table. Shuffled and dealt them there on the couch. He was rusty on the rules, needed some instruction. She beat him once, then dealt another hand. What was it that he was expecting from this game? That he would relax enough to tell her about his day at work or about the academic achievements of his children, and that she would report that she had walked to the gas station to pick up her newspaper, but that soon the mosquitoes would barely let her leave the house? The magazines said that new dynamics emerged when family members set aside tasks and distractions and intentionally spent time together. Relationships were renewed and deepened, they said. But she did not need him to tell her that he had loved the crippled neighbor more than he loved her daughter, and she had no desire to tell him that she hated the woods, which always threatened to swallow her just as they had swallowed her orange tabby shortly after her arrival. What good could come of such a conversation?

No, she knew better than Martin that these visits were dependent upon the distraction of the television, as well as on his need to revisit the past, to whatever he'd done here that she did not care to think about. And so she had not been surprised that day when his attention faltered in the middle of the second hand.

He had no practice in participating in activities with other people. No doubt at home he only observed games from behind a newspaper, if they played anything there at all—she did not know. As he waited for her to make her play, she saw his eyes stray to the television screen. A little while later, he again had to be prompted to take his turn. In perhaps one of the few gentle and discreet moments of her adult life, she made a small joke about the scene they were both watching, then pretended to become quickly engrossed in the part that followed. "You won't believe that guy," she said, pointing to the funny man who was the main character. She reached forward to raise the volume, laying her cards face-up on the coffee table as she did as if simply absent-minded. Then she settled into the story.

They had never tried to play again, and unless she gave him some chore that she could not do for herself, they simply sat on the couch watching television together, as they did now. She had once done more, surely—a little cooking, a little cleaning, caring for the cat that had slept beside her in bed since her husband's death and that never left the yard when they lived in town. But after their arrival in the woods, her cat always seemed taken with some great adventure out of doors, returning ragged and beaten. One morning she awakened not to the purring of her cat, but to a squirming pile of maggots, as if her husband's corpse had reappeared in the form of dust and worms. The cat was in the kitchen, trying to clean a wound from a fight. Once she fed him, he begged to be let out, and she had, against her better instincts, done so. The cat never returned. What had he wanted so badly that he would be compelled to leave safety for danger? Trade comfort for suffering?

Without the company of the cat, she eventually felt that her loyalties lay with the television. The actors and the plot and the electronic hum were more reliable than these visits from her son-in-law, who after long silence now interrupted the show.

"Maggie didn't say anything at all about my parents?" he asked, trying to keep the curiosity out of his voice.

Annette shook her head. "We talked about my bad marriage and my dead husband's pinky finger." After a pause she said pointedly, "That was all we talked about." She chuckled along with the laugh track, then, as if they were still on the subject of Maggie's employment, said, "Probably for the best, this move to the city." She crushed her cigarette in the ash tray. "What can you give her? No neighbors, no kin. Just the walking dead."

CHAPTER TWELVE

Hannah was pulling her nightgown over her head when she heard the faint cry of a cat somewhere behind her. She turned, letting her gown fall to the floor, but could see nothing. She'd not thought about the cat today, not when she returned from the library or any time after, assuming that wherever Maggie was, that was where the cat would be. And she had, admittedly, not thought much about where Maggie was either, since it was easiest just to pretend that she had already gone. Now, as Hannah moved across the room to peer around the far side of the bed, she heard faint noises from behind her husband's bureau. She stopped, suppressing a cry. She did not want to disturb the children. Holding her breath, she listened, but the sound retreated and died.

In the silence that followed, Hannah's heart did not slow. She waited, eyes resting on the brown glass letter holder on top of her husband's dresser. She had always found the empty letter holder unreasonably irksome—a useless object of beauty—especially after her husband gave her special instructions not to dust it for fear of its getting broken. At some point she'd stopped seeing it at all.

When no more sounds came from behind the wall, she crossed the corner of the room and entered the tiny half bath. The pedestal sink hunkered in the shadows just inside the door opposite the toilet. In the full-length mirror on the far wall Hannah saw herself illuminated from behind by the lamp on her nightstand, thin and hunched in her long gown. Brown spots scattered over the beveled glass that had begun to warp and waver, yet instead of absorbing the reality that the mirror reflected back to her, Hannah saw the illusion of escape. She stepped forward and put her palms against the cold glass, then ran one thumb along the edge of peeling brown wallpaper that met with the heavy wooden frame. She leaned against it, but it did not give. She leaned a little harder, and then harder still. From within she felt a click similar to the click of the medicine cabinet above the bathroom sink. When she let go again, the framed mirror swung out like a door.

The space behind the mirror was larger than she had imagined in her not imagining—in her dim awareness of some kind of recess that she had never explored, a musty malfunction in construction. In heeding her mother's advice that men needed a retreat for whiskey and pornography to keep them from wandering the streets at night, Hannah mostly envisioned her husband simply withdrawing to the bathroom to smoke his pipe in the dark with the window open. Yet here was a whole, secret room not much smaller than Maggie's, bathed in moonlight from the circular window Hannah had noticed earlier in the day. When her eyes adjusted, she found the electrical switch to her left and turned on a naked bulb hanging from the ceiling. A twin bed against the wall must have been there before they bought the house as, she supposed, the book case against the wall on the right had also been. She did not know when he discovered this spot.

In front of the window, a round plate of stained glass hung by chains from the ceiling, forming purple mountains, a yellow sun, and blue sky. At the base of the mountains the hills became green, with a dark blue stream running beside a brown cabin with white smoke emanating from its chimney. Even though the picture had not been placed right against the window, it would still catch the light, shining out for everyone below to see or to not see, as they chose. To her it seemed an oddly dull and empty landscape, full of archetypes without detail, picturesque in form but otherwise vacant. In moving to this farmhouse to start a family, Hannah had envisioned the kind of work that refreshed and restored. She would, she thought, embrace a cycle of routine chores in rhythm with the seasons, as her in-laws did, growing and then preparing food, adorning her home with flowers, going to town to exchange news with neighbors in summer, retreating for the short days of winter. And in the middle of this practical business, she would have books for stimulation and the challenge of academic projects for her children. As with any imaginings, she had worked only from still images or, at best, short scenes of the kind in books. But the books had not helped her to anticipate that between the moments of satisfaction—when she broke the soil with her shovel to settle the frame for the raised bed or nursed her first child—she would continue to carry the weight of her own consciousness, which would find the attention to detail needed for the garden tedious, the long quiet nights by the woodstove draining, the partial exile from town social life disorienting, the equally partial participation in town social life suffocating. Boredom became the only truth—wasn't all of life dull, in its superficial distinctions? One had to live someplace, do something, love someone. Even her reading disappointed, as

Hannah came to understand that authors wrote the kinds of things that interested them in such a way—persuasively—that they might captivate others, and then others took them too seriously. Took the messages and dictates for right living too seriously, or took the sad turns and dark thoughts as prophecy for their own lives, which they might otherwise live quite contentedly. Novels in particular, with all of their morbid focus on what happens at the end, had caused her to depend on the ending of her own story to clarify the argument of all the preceding chapters—that love was possible, that healing and renewal reclaimed lives, or that everything was in an inevitable state of degeneration and unraveling—as if from her deathbed she could look back and decide then and only then what to believe about her own life, evaluating the recurring images and central themes for the appropriate messages, telling her what to believe just at the time that it no longer mattered.

Still, she might be able to recover some appetite for life if she could remain in this empty room, sleeping on the bed, accessing other parts of the house by the stairs that she now spotted and down which the cat must have disappeared. The stairs were her only real surprise, something that no part of her mind had guessed at during all these years when she thought that whatever her husband did when he slipped out of bed at night he did alone, irregularly, a small indulgence that at some point he'd given up. Sometime after Edwin was born her reliable deep sleep had given way to something fitful, her twilight dreams always crowded with noises—a child's sigh, an off-key hymn, a gasp and then a grunt, the click of a flashlight, the sharp shut of an oven door, the slap of flesh, a wail for lost love ripping through the night from one direction and a keening for a lost son from the other—a cacophony that kept her from ever really getting rest. Yet she had never heard the creak of these wooden stairs. She shut the stairwell door now because she did not want to think about the room connecting to other places, but simply as a space that was waiting to be filled by her, untouched by others. She could claim it for her own. Now that her husband wasn't using it anymore, she could disappear here.

Seeing the window earlier today, then, had been a gift, she thought as she sank onto the thin mattress, which squeaked beneath her. That afternoon, surveying her son's labor, she had looked past him to the unfamiliar window in the corner of the house and felt a series of bolts and locks unclick, as if she held the water of a canal that was only just now rushing out to sea. From the grapevine where she retreated, the green glass had caught the light and glinted a little. She hadn't been so far into the backyard in years. When she left the house, she always went toward town, toward the relief that was so brief and fleeting that she could barely recognize it for what it was, tainted with something else—self-consciousness and shame. But her son—her children—they were back here all the time. With the exception of Maggie, they lived out here in the summer months. If asked about the window, what would they say? They would look at her in disdain, indicating that surely she knew better than to ask such an absurd question.

Now, sitting on the bare, striped mattress, she saw that the room had come into existence just when she needed it to. She felt she'd even called it into existence, just as her husband must have done out of need that had nothing to do with her and that she would never understand. And now it was her turn. She, too, had needs that he would never understand. And one of those was to be away from him. She would take down the stained glass, which troubled her as the letter holder did, for reasons she could not quite identify. Eventually, when the children were ready, she would go to and from the kitchen and the downstairs bathroom without ever having to squeeze by him on the central stairs again. He would be like a boarder at her private bed and breakfast. A traveler whose business was not her own. Her mistake had been in ever thinking of him as anything else. He would give her this room because he owed her. She had suspected for nearly a decade that he owed her, and was strangely pleased to find she'd been right—he had been hoarding something and would now have to share. What an odd feeling—to be right after so much doubt! It was a kind of gift, seeing her rightness in this instance.

She stood and crossed the room. At the bookshelf, she was taken aback to see the neatly folded mechanic's jumpsuit that had been her father's. Her husband had not worn it in years. She reached out to touch the rough polyester, remembering her father wearing it as he worked beneath the hoods of cars that he bought to fix and resell. As a child, she stood beside the car to hand him his tools, a heady desperate waiting during which she might receive a compliment for being so helpful. She remained wide open for these compliments as if practicing a childhood spiritual discipline. They came just often enough to nourish expectations that stubbornly survived the much more frequent criticisms. *Just how much affirmation do you need?* her husband had once asked her, as if wanting to be flooded with warmth was some kind of moral failing. What did anyone ever want but generous portions of kindness, and if not that then at least consistency? Even reliable meanness that you could build a wall against to dismiss the person altogether, move on to other possibilities. But her father had kept her guessing, and though he had been dead for years, she felt herself guessing still.

Hannah picked up a book. A tiffany lamp glowed on the glossy cover. She hesitated before flipping open the book filled with patterns for stained glass. She well remembered how eagerly her husband had watched their new neighbor's demonstration at the town craft festival, and how he asked more questions about the process when they stopped over to welcome the couple to town. When within a year this neighbor divorced and moved away, her husband fell into sudden mourning, revealing an attachment she'd never seen before and that, when she finally asked, he could not explain. *I don't know very many interesting men, I suppose,* he said at last. *All the men at work are dull, the same.* He spoke as though in gentle confession before making it clear that she was not to mention the subject again. But she had no intention of ever mentioning the subject again, all of her courage exhausted in this first and only effort.

She put the book back on the shelf alongside the other books that she now hesitated to examine. She might simply return to her bedroom. In the morning, she could ask her husband to put all of his things from the room into a box to take to work or throw out. She could still have what she wanted, after all, taking over the room for her own uses without further discussion. She had no doubt that her husband would give her what she asked for, and in imagining his compliance on this if not other subjects, she felt a small surge of tenderness. She nearly turned away then, but the crocheted hammock on the cover of one of the other books caught her attention, calling forth fond memories of his creative phase, when he learned to macramé for the express purpose of building the children a play area among the cedar trees. She picked up the book of knotting, glancing at the photographs and the instructions, recalling the contentment that this evening occupation had brought to him and therefore to them all, as the family read around him and she fed the woodstove.

In lingering over these memories she forgot her foreboding, and was therefore unprepared when she picked up a book with a black and white picture of a nude man on the cover. His head was tilted down, muscles taut and skin smooth, his spine and buttocks making the letter C. She stared at the photograph for a long while, supposing the book to be in the same artistic category as the books of macramé and stained glass. After all, she reminded herself, she had half-expected naked photographs to be the central feature of this hidden place. Then, because the man on the cover was beautiful and the photograph was beautiful and she had not seen anything so beautiful in some time, she took a deep breath and opened the book. In flipping through the pages, she saw that all of the photographs in the book were of handsome nude men. She gazed at picture after picture, seeing without any effort at all the artfulness of the long penis, the smooth chest, and the broad shoulders. When the sadness finally came, it first came as grief that these men had been withheld from her, all of that untouched beauty that she might at one time have sought out or demanded contained in her bursting heart.

When she failed to see anything but the beckoning, taunting member, she tore the first page from the book and began to shred it on the floor. She hated to shred the picture of the stunning man whose qualities she savored, but he was looking through her at someone else, had been looking through her at someone else for quite some time, and so she found shredding the picture brought more satisfaction than she might have anticipated. She ripped picture after picture out of the book, wondering how it was that she'd never before appreciated the pleasure of destruction. With trembling hands, she considered what else might need shredding, what else might call for shaking or shattering or singeing when she was finished here.

From the other rooms, the children heard sobs crash like breaking glass against the hard bottom of their dreams.

* * * *

Thursday morning Maggie awoke on the bench with the sense that someone was standing over her. She opened her eyes and sat up, turning in time to see the runner's shoulders disappearing down the stairs. Phillip had once used the sixteen steep steps to build strength and endurance, but their mother found the noise tiresome and so for quite some time Maggie had not seen him upstairs at all. And yet from the privacy of her own bedroom, how would she know what any of them did at the odd hours?

She sat up, aware of having slept better for yesterday's long walk. The landing was bright, yet the house was strangely quiet, with both bedroom doors still shut. As in a dream Maggie felt she had heard her mother crying, and a man crying as well, but her father's car had not been in the driveway when she arrived home the night before, and she had never wakened to his footsteps on the stairs. Whatever he did in the city once a week, he did it neatly, with regularity. He didn't stumble in at an unpredictable hour. He drove up on time, satisfied, presumably, in some form that was tidy, uncomplicated, and

not too expensive, and then on Thursday morning was up as usual
without the suggestion of either an extra kick or an extra weight to
his step. Last night his absence had seemed fortuitous—he might
not find their mother out of bed after all, as if the only threat was
each becoming aware of what the others knew, even though Maggie
herself did not know what there was to know, exactly. Only that
something had changed during the night while their mother lurked
in a forgotten room, and was perhaps changing still. The house was
gaining knowledge of itself.

Maggie bent to push on her boots, remembering as she did that
she'd left yesterday's clothes on the line—they would be dew-soaked
by now. She smoothed the gray dress she had slept in, the front skirt
covered with bits of melted chocolate and pulls in the fabric from
her trip through the woods. The dresses were a problem—she could
rotate the two only so long, and then there would be Sunday, when it
would be best to have a third. Suddenly so many women were within
reach from whom she might beg or borrow—her grandmothers,
Mamie, the receptionist, the neighbors in town. The landscape felt
cluttered with people who knew a little something about her, from
whom she might ask a favor. Yet she already felt she owed all of them
something—an explanation, an apology, a disclaimer?

When Maggie stood to fold her coverlet, a sparkle of color caught
her eye from the north window. Peering into the sunshine, she was
astonished to once again see a cluster of balloons, this time purple
and gold, half-buried within a cloud of green leaves. Surely this
neighbor with such an eye for color would be the best person to ask
for a discarded dress, no matter that the terms of their relationship
were still new and uncertain. Like the raised red flag of a mailbox,

the balloons seemed to promise that the receptionist would be home.

Once in the kitchen, Maggie pulled a biscuit from the jar and sliced it open, spreading it with soft butter from a dish on the counter. As she chewed, she listened for the theologian, who like everyone else in the house, appeared to be sleeping. She considered waking him, telling him of her errand, but not even Warren had inquired of her whereabouts the night before. Yet he'd met her in the kitchen when she arrived breathless from running, with Lula just appearing from behind the open basement door.

"She's been in the basement this whole time?" Maggie had said, closing the screen behind her and bending to pet the cat wrapped around her boots.

"She must have somehow got behind the paneling," he said. "I've not seen her until now."

"She'll be hungry, the poor thing," Maggie said.

"She's been fed," he said flatly, retrieving the water bowl from the stairs and closing the basement door. He was tired, or irritable. She smiled at him, grateful. She felt irresponsible—she'd not intended to be gone for so long. When Warren did not immediately retreat to his room as expected, Maggie hesitated, then whispered, "Father's car." She did not know how to ask the question, but was determined to speak.

The theologian shrugged as he had done when she saw him in the woods with his brother. The shrug, she suddenly realized, indicated that he knew more than he seemed to. She felt she could say, *Our mother is in a hidden place upstairs*, and he would simply nod and shrug. She considered saying, *Our grandparents live nearby,* but her brother was already turning to leave the kitchen, shuffling back to his room like a put-upon gatekeeper, roused from sleep by late travelers. Perhaps he had been alarmed by her indirect inquiry. They were both ill-equipped for such an exchange. They were also both uneasy, lest their mother should descend, needing something from them that neither was prepared to give. Lest their father should return, finding them out of bed as if they knew something unusual was occurring, creating the obligation for someone to speak or act.

Now Maggie put chicken livers in a bowl for Lula, who would have just been let out by Phillip. She decided against rousing Warren. She would leave her brother to the collective effort that the family would have to put forth when they could not lie abed any longer, when they would have to come out to pretend not to have listened late for their father's footsteps on the stairs, not to have heard their mother crying. As for Maggie, she wanted this process to be completed while she was gone, so she could assess the end result from a safe distance. Everyone else wanted the same thing—her father, who might never have come home; the runner, up and out early; the rest of the family, sleeping on in hopes that some transformation would occur while they were without consciousness. Maggie had shepherded much in the house, perhaps even including these latest changes, but she did not have to be there to witness it all, as if it were a design of her own making.

Just outside the kitchen, Lula was licking her paws a few feet from a dead mouse. Maggie rubbed her head, then placed the bowl before her and set out through the backyard for the woods. Whatever fears she'd had when running from the creek last night receded with the daylight—surely she had simply been startled by an animal rustling in the reeds, and not a person at all. Her grandmothers, with their vague and coded messages about tramps and other things, had unnerved her.

Yet Maggie had been walking on the path through the rho-dodendron for only a few minutes when she saw a bulky frame approaching her from the opposite direction. She stopped, startled by the advance of a stranger whom she did not expect to see on a path she too quickly assumed was used only by her brothers. In a moment, she recognized the prowling man from Mamie's house, his unblinking gaze trained on her. Uncertain of the etiquette for passing along a narrow path in the woods, she stepped to one side of the trail, hoping he would simply nod and walk on by.

"It's the long-legged colt!" he said, stopping before her. He reached up to wipe the sweat dripping from his forehead.

"Good morning," Maggie said formally, stepping up onto the bank to signal that he should pass.

"On the contrary! Ladies first." He did not move to give her room. "I've just returned from the market," he said, "where I sold three cakes and left a fourth on our good neighbor's doorstep. And you? What's your business?"

Maggie hesitated, instinctively searching for an excuse that might put her in the company of another. "I'm catching up with my brother," she said. "He should be just ahead." As soon as she spoke, she realized she would be caught in her lie, as had her brother indeed come this way, it was likely the man would have passed him as well.

To her dismay, however, the man winked and said, "Ah, then you're not all that far behind. Like father like son, they say." He reached out a hand as if to touch her shoulder. "And what does the sister like, then?"

She stepped away into the vines. "I'm sorry?" she said.

"I've been to the market to sell cakes," he said, hand dropping back by his side. "Pink cakes with white icing." He stared at her a moment, the smile fading, his voice dropping to a whisper. "I love to lick the icing," he said, "but it's the cake inside I'm really after."

Maggie quickly brushed past him, and as she did, he bent down and slid his fingertips across the exposed calf between her skirt and boot. When she began to run, he chuckled deeply. She heard the laughter recede, fading as she ran, but did not stop running until she reached the edge of the woods, where she shot out into the meadow and then stopped to search the tree line behind her. She waited, heart pounding, ready to run up the stairs to the house at a moment's notice, but the man did not come.

Quickly crossing the last stretch of meadow, Maggie was relieved to see that the receptionist's front door was partly opened—she was not at work then. Maggie could take refuge here for a while and find a safer way home. She climbed the flight of stairs slowly, catching her breath, watching the purple and gold balloons spiral above the porch, their ribbons once again tucked beneath the plant pot. When she reached the top step, she saw that a white cake box sat on the table, lid open, a fork thrust deep inside where the receptionist had eaten straight from the box. Across the porch pink crumbs trailed, already attracting ants. Maggie did not go any closer to the box, as if peering in would give the old man a glimpse inside of her. Instead she was anxious to tell the receptionist what had happened and to ask what should be done about it, about having such a man in the woods, crossing the edge of her family's property where her sisters played near the mulberry tree.

Approaching the door, Maggie was about to knock when she realized she could hear the receptionist's voice. She listened carefully, trying to understand what she could in advance, as she now felt she had the right to do, no longer walking blindly into uncertain territory. The receptionist was talking excitedly and at length, but Maggie could hear only the intonations and not the words, rapid syllables receding and advancing around short pauses and giggles. For a moment Maggie thought of her lonely grandmother whom she'd imagined to be speaking to the refrigerator the night before, but then the end of the sentence lifted as if in a question. After a pause, a boy answered quietly with a voice that Maggie recognized: her brother had indeed preceded her on the path. The receptionist seemed encouraged by his response, and spoke at length in return, her voice softening, slowing, prodding. Maggie understood that the mood had shifted, and that this—these shifts in moods and these compliments and expressions and exclamations—was why her brother had come, why he had abandoned the cake for the tea, and why the tea would be abandoned, too, sweet as it was, leaving him free to drink in the words that here were available in such abundance and excess, flowing in response to the slightest pressure.

Maggie turned from the door and sat on the top stair, stunned and breathless again. She looked across the porch to the balloons twisting in the breeze, seeing them now as a playful signal not intended for her, though she had foolishly followed the summons twice now, as if her own name had been inscribed against the sky. And yet she could also imagine that the receptionist might have wanted any one of them who was willing, an object to curl up against in a house without furniture. Maggie should leave, yet she was unwilling to enter the woods, where the man might lie in wait. She had avoided the woods for many years and now saw that she should have continued avoiding them—she'd gained nothing from her explorations except knowledge of a world she had been prepared to leave. At this moment all she wanted was for her brother—who had also gone places he should not have gone—to walk her home.

So she waited, having some idea that she could pretend to have just arrived, to have received no answer to her knock, and to be politely catching her breath on the stairs. Along the brick storm drain in the side yard the brown hemlock needles were piled high. Maggie had been tossed over the dead son's shoulder there. She had wanted moments like that, being tossed over an older boy's shoulder, being pushed along in a wheel barrow, until she suddenly wanted no more moments like that, at some time she could not recall but could still be thankful for—a clarity of vision that kept her from the foolish blindness of the receptionist, who craved what was not hers; of the fat lady, whose new man would rob her as much as her husband must have done; of her father's mother, keeping poor company with the meaningless chatter inside her mind; of her mother's mother, shrunk and embalmed like a discarded fingertip; and of her own mother, who in childbearing hoped to become a beloved adult but could not nurse enough to nourish some dry thirst of her own. And yet in growing up to defy them all, Maggie had also misplaced the flaming of desire that was briefly conjured in the children's room and that at some point came to depend on an object for its existence—an object she could not create through imagination alone.

Sometime later, Maggie heard the door behind her swing open, then the creaking hinges stopped abruptly. She stayed facing forward as if lost in a daydream until, after a prolonged pause, she heard the back door open just as the front door closed again—her brother would not be walking her home after all, as she should have guessed. She felt she was coming to the end of pretense, but she did her part to participate a little longer, belatedly turning to face the receptionist as if she'd simply been admiring the view. It was the best performance she could give and the receptionist would have to be satisfied with it.

"Maggie!" the receptionist said. "How lovely to see you." She took a chair, crossing her legs beneath a long blue robe. Her feet were bare, toenails painted plum. "I'm sorry not to be more presentably dressed—it's my morning to go in late. Have you been here long?"

"No," Maggie said, standing. "I got winded on the way and thought I would catch my breath before knocking."

"I understand—the stairs are a terrible bother. I suppose you noticed that I had a cake delivery." The receptionist took up the fork and popped a bite into her mouth. She spoke politely, casually, but Maggie could hear the distraction in her voice. Two days ago, the receptionist had seemed genuinely glad to see her. If hers was a false warmth, reserved now for Phillip alone, then Maggie could not help but also doubt the more ambivalent welcomes from the other neighbors, from kin, and from the church director in the city. Where might she be wanted?

"I do so love cake for breakfast—just the sheer abandon of it," the receptionist said. "Would you like a piece? I can get you a plate."

"I've just had breakfast, but thank you." Maggie knew that she should explain why she had come, but she had no desire to ask for a dress now. "Lula caught a mouse this morning," she said feebly.

"Did she now? I never cease to be amazed. I've missed her. If you don't mind, please do bring her back. Say Sunday afternoon. Surely now your father can see the advantages of having a cat."

But her father was not at home. "I'm going to the city," Maggie said, and her voice sounded higher than usual. "I have a job in the city. I leave tomorrow. I can't bring her back."

"Well there's no need to keep repeating yourself," the receptionist said, still picking at the cake. "You've not left yet, so there's no reason to keep assuming that you will." She paused, smiling thinly. "But if you do, then just send Lula back with one of the others." She raised an eyebrow, adding, "Phillip, perhaps?"

Maggie did not reply. She turned and took a step down the stairs, then hesitated, staring at the woods.

"Do you feel unwell?" the receptionist asked, standing and closing the cake box. "You look like you've seen a ghost."

"Just a tramp," Maggie said, her voice low.

"Well, I wouldn't go so far as that," the receptionist laughed.

Maggie said nothing.

"Come now," the receptionist said. "Surely you're old enough. I like visitors. I like having company."

"I meant that I've seen tramps in the woods," Maggie said shakily. "Last night. And again this morning on the way here. The woods are not safe."

The receptionist combed her hair with her fingers. "Well, I can't imagine they'd do you any harm," she said, sounding rather bored. "Most of the time vagrants just want someplace to sleep, without any trouble."

"It was Mamie's companion I saw," Maggie said.

The receptionist laughed. "The cake delivery man? Then you've even less to worry about than I thought. He's perverse, no doubt, but I would hardly take him seriously."

Maggie did not speak, understanding that if some might say the world she inhabited was small and protected, this world had also been precarious and uncertain and at times treacherous.

"I've got to get to work now, or of course I'd take you home, since you've clearly had a bit of a scare," the receptionist said, crossing the porch to retrieve the balloons. "Your brothers spotted my first set of balloons only a month or so ago, when I tied them to a tree in the meadow, right on their regular path to the market. I secured a little card to the bottom, inviting them up for tea. Clever of me, don't you think? Just for fun—a little diversion." She wrapped the ribbons around her fingers, adding, "I'd often hoped that your other brother would also come along, instead of waiting at the bottom of the stairs, drooping and alone. The both of them—all of you—starved for better options."

Maggie did not speak. People had made a habit of sharing their inmost thoughts with her, as if she had nothing at stake.

"Of course it's best not to tell anyone about your brother's visits," the receptionist said, turning toward the door. "I understand that your parents have rules about so many things, or so your brother hints. But he doesn't have to explain that your father never wants anyone to have what he can't have himself. I've known that for years. Still, your brother's a bit young, after all, and people can so easily misunderstand." She paused, tilting her head as she gazed at Maggie. "But then, it's not really in your nature to tell, is it? No one's told anything in your house for years."

CHAPTER THIRTEEN

The children's room was divided. Two days ago, Quinn had hoped that a new unification was occurring, beginning when they rescued Maggie from sleeping in their mother's bed and building the next day when they worked together to make the secret trip to the fat lady's house. Now he was squatting alone in the grass beside the storm cellar, waiting on the others, worried that there would be trouble.

He hadn't liked the fat lady—she stared at him with eyes made huge behind her thick glasses, and when he sat in her kitchen with his feet on the rung of the stool, eating a cupcake, she suddenly placed her teeth around his exposed kneecap and breathed a hot laugh there. His younger brother had smiled. Quinn could see by the look on Edwin's face that he'd known this would happen and had not warned him. As for the fat lady, she looked at his fingers frozen in the act of peeling back the wrapper, and giggled until she had to take off her glasses to wipe her eyes.

Quinn might have been angry at his brother for laughing at him had the fat lady not turned from his now damp knee toward his brother, who smiled, ready to pay his dues. Instead of clamping her mouth around his knee, however, the woman turned her wide frame and sat herself down on his brother's small lap. She did so with grandeur and drama, lifting her skirt and apron as if she were intending to have a long comfortable chat with a friend, folding her hands in her lap as she settled herself. Edwin was on the lower stool, his feet on the floor, which made it possible for her to place her weight there, balancing and humming as if she did not know that he existed. Quinn watched his brother's smile drain and his face go pale—Edwin clearly had never experienced this particular treatment before. Quinn took no pleasure in seeing his brother suffer, not even in revenge, but he found that he could not speak in order to help him. Finally Edwin gasped, "Get up," as if she had been sitting on his lungs.

"Say please," she said, clearly enjoying herself.

He'd whispered the word and she stood, returning to her baking counter. "Now off you go!" she said with a smile. "And tell your sisters I've never seen a more cowardly pair in all my life."

But his sisters hadn't cared, and this morning, when the four of them awakened sad and uneasy from a collective dream, they were still careful and kind with one another. They spoke in whispers as they waited for their mother to rouse them, and when she did not do so, they took Bertie and made their way from the biscuit jar to the spider web. They ignored the unsettling doubt over their mother's belated rising, behaving as if on a holiday.

Yet just as they were deciding what game they might like to play, Douglas and his friend had showed up again, just as they had the day before.

"You've got to see this," Douglas said when he appeared by the spider web, hands shoved in his pockets. "We've got something to show you."

"Aren't you supposed to be mowing the lawn or something?" Agnes asked, clearly hoping to dismiss them both right away.

"Oh, so you've been down into the cellar?" Douglas taunted. Everyone in the hammock grew still, as if they were victims of a real spider web and had ceased to struggle.

"What cellar?" Agnes asked. She should have continued to feign indifference, Quinn had thought. He looked around for Maggie but she was nowhere to be seen.

"The storm cellar of the house, of course," Douglas said. "It's unlocked. Sean found the key in the door." His friend towered over them looking bored and smug. And why else had he come back except to do such things? To tower over them in contempt?

"You're lying," Agnes said, then pretended to yawn. Douglas was intruding where he did not belong, the yawn said. He shouldn't be playing with the babies.

"Dad says that the door always stays locked," Douglas said. "He's the one who's lying. There's a key in it right now."

With a sinking feeling, Quinn felt the tenuousness of their connection to the outside world—everything that he didn't understand that could not be explained. Someone had found the key and broken into the cellar—some tramp who might be there right now, waiting. None of them wanted to explore the forbidden cellar, but none of them wanted to appear afraid to do so, either, not just because they needed to seem brave in front of the older boy for the sake of braveness, but because showing even the smallest bit of fear might provoke larger threats. There were no adults about now, no one who might protect them from Douglas and the older boy, from whatever game they might force everyone else to play, whatever punishment they might impose if the mood seized them.

Agnes hesitated. "Who cares?" she said. "It's just a cellar."

"Shows what you know," Douglas said. "I just went inside. There's a secret passage. It leads somewhere. To the house, I think." He pulled his hand from his pocket and waved a flashlight in front of her.

"You think. But you're too scared to go alone."

"Are you?"

Quinn felt then—they all did—how Agnes had backed herself into a corner. She looked up at Douglas, and Quinn could see in her face the sorrow of concession.

Agnes sighed and ran one hand down her smooth ponytail. "I guess we can see where it goes." She looked around at the others. "This will be a dangerous mission," she said without conviction. Her older brother scoffed and the neighbor boy chuckled. She turned and gave them a cold look. She was going to explore with them, wasn't she? Well then let her do it her own way.

"Ellen, you'll need to stay with Bertie in the spider web." Ellen nodded, looking relieved. She hated dark places and cave crickets. She believed in ghosts. Bertie cuddled up closer to her. "Edwin and Quinn, come with us."

Quinn anguished over the separation of the group, the morning's comfort evaporating. When the five of them arrived at the cellar door, Douglas told Agnes to try it, as if she needed to feel the door ease open herself to believe that it was not locked, in spite of the skeleton key with the dangling wooden key chain. She did, and the battered door swung open. Douglas reached up and pulled on a cord just inside the entrance. The light was feeble, the shadows inside barely receding.

"We'll have to close the door behind us," Douglas said to Edwin, "so you'll stand guard at the base of these stairs." Edwin nodded and Douglas turned to Quinn, "And you stand guard on the outside."

"Stand guard?" Agnes said, rolling her eyes.

"We need a lookout," Douglas said. "In case Phillip comes—"

"I saw him jogging on my way over here," Sean said. "He was headed up the ridge."

"Okay, then in case Mom comes."

"Or Maggie," Quinn said quietly.

"Maggie?" Douglas scoffed, as if Quinn was invoking a lesser god, or a disillusioned superhero who hadn't made an appearance in years. "If you hear anyone approach," Douglas said to Quinn, "knock on the door. That will alert Edwin, who will come and find us in the passageway."

Quinn crossed his arms and turned from them, secretly relieved he'd been given the outside job because he was not considered as brave as his younger brother. In the next instant, Douglas stepped toward the door, ducked his head beneath the frame, and disappeared down the steps. Sean followed him, sending a last wicked grin over his shoulder to Quinn. When Agnes hesitated, Douglas urged her on from below. After a moment, she covered her head with her hands because the cave crickets that lined the ceiling were scattering at their passing. Edwin stared expressionless at Quinn, then pulled the door shut behind him. After a moment, Lula came circling from around the cellar and rubbed against his legs.

And so Quinn became the lookout, nervously squatting or standing for some time now with clumps of clover in his hands, both afraid and hopeful that his mother would appear at the backdoor in her nightdress. Instead, Maggie emerged from the woods. He felt a flood of gratitude, for she would have been his first choice for rescue, no matter how excluded she might have been in these last three days. Agnes had told him that he was silly for assuming their father had punished Maggie by sending her to the woods—she wasn't forbidden to come in the house, Agnes said—but how else to explain that every time they went to bed at night or rose in the morning she was out of doors, leaving, returning? And yesterday, when for once she tried to join them in their play, they had banished her from the war zone. Seeing her now, he knew that he would neglect his duties, that he was already doing so in not turning immediately to warn Edwin, just as the others might have known he would had they given the possibility of adult intrusion any real consideration.

As she passed through the archway toward him, however, Quinn became conflicted by split loyalties and did not move to welcome her after all. Instead he sat down in the grass, thinking this might appear more natural. Lula climbed into his lap, and for a moment he simply lost himself in the pleasure of her soft fur against his bare legs.

* * * *

Because Maggie's fear of the man in the woods receded as she reached the backyard without incident, she was able to see her little brother pale with apprehension, sitting cross-legged near the storm cellar door, chin in fist. He had never been a good actor. Never disguised his feelings well. She glanced through the screen door as she passed the kitchen, but saw no one there. A new anxiety began to curl inside her. She hadn't expected to find the children outside—not this time of morning when they were usually completing their lessons.

"Where's Mother?" she asked when she reached him. He looked

up at her, his brown curls ruffled. She longed to lay his head in her lap as she had sometimes done.

Quinn glanced over at the house, then shrugged and resumed petting the cat. Maggie looked up at the round window, where this morning, at least, the light was not catching green glass. Quinn followed her gaze, taking in the window that none of them ever looked at or spoke of. When Maggie looked back at him, she saw that his eyes were wide with fear.

"The girls—no one's gone to see the fat lady, have they?"

Quinn's eyes grew bigger, surprised that she knew about this secret, but then he remembered the cupcake wrapper—she'd been there herself. "No," he whispered.

Maggie sighed, relieved. She should have stayed home to see whether their mother would take charge. Now she could see that the children were scattered—a bad sign. Quinn, never one to linger long alone, was possibly on the verge of tears, unwilling to tell her something lest he betray someone else. She sat down beside him.

"Where are the others?" she asked.

He looked petrified, then waved in the direction of the hammock. "Ellen is in the spider web," he said, "with Bertie."

"Bertie?" She'd not pictured the youngest venturing out, which now appeared foolish and naïve.

Quinn nodded.

"And the others?"

He shrugged again. She saw him glance toward the cellar door. Inserted in the lock was a long metal key that she had never seen before. She was close enough to reach out and touch the flat piece of wood dangling from the key by a chain. On each side was a postage stamp featuring a cardinal and a mockingbird, lacquered to a soft gleam to keep the stamps from peeling off. She recognized the keychain as something one of the older boys had made years ago as a father's day gift, an art project completed at the dining room table.

"They found it there," Quinn said, seeing her staring at the key. He was afraid she would think they'd rummaged through their father's things. "It was already unlocked. They said there's a passage."

Maggie said nothing, aware of a blank spot on the mental map she'd been creating these last few days as she circled the property. She had followed the creek threading between fields and woods, the trails winding from house to house, the hallways connecting empty rooms to stairways that lead to places of retreat and exile. Yet there had also been unseen pathways, places rats and even cats could find, places that were easily accessible while wildly out of reach, and so she was now able to anticipate, in crude and rough form, that there might be a connection between the cellar below and the room with the round window above.

She reached out for Quinn's cold soft fingertips. He was upset by his deception, and she would try to comfort him before she went into the cellar herself. Lula purred loudly between them.

"I went to see the cupcake lady yesterday," he said without prompting, and she understood that this was a confession, that he wanted everything to be known just as the cellar excursion was now known.

"And how did you like your cupcake?" Maggie asked.

"I didn't like her laughing on my knee," he said. "Has she ever done that to you?"

Maggie nodded. "A long time ago when I was your age," she said. "I didn't much like it, either."

"I don't think I like cupcakes," he said, as if in admission of failure.

"What flavor did you eat?"

"Red velvet, she called it."

"I've not had it myself, that I recall."

"It was all she had," Quinn admitted. "Edwin loved it."

"There are other flavors. You've no idea how many."

He looked mildly reassured that life's promises hadn't shrunk in his first venture out into the world. She leaned toward him, anxious not to delay too long. "I've got to go find the others now," she whispered.

Quinn began to cry. "Edwin is down there. So is Agnes. But what if there are rats?" Maggie saw that Agnes was braver than she herself had been, neglecting her opportunity to investigate two days ago when she left her parents' room in such haste, startled by memory. Had she not done so, she might have been able to protect her siblings from whatever the hidden room had to offer.

She leaned forward to kiss Quinn on the forehead, understanding that he did not want to say Douglas was in charge. She remembered with some concern his play with the older boy yesterday. But surely the neighbor had not come to visit two days in a row, and though Douglas could be harsh with his younger siblings, he wasn't cruel. She stood. "They'll be fine," she reassured Quinn. "I'll find them." She opened the door to the cellar, and after a moment of adjusting to the shadows, saw Edwin sitting on an egg crate at the base of the stairs, clutching his knees.

"Come here," she said, her voice echoing slightly.

He stood and climbed the stairs without hesitation, glancing toward one corner of the cellar as if afraid the others would return at his moment of betrayal. When he reached the door where Maggie was standing, she said, "The two of you should go get Ellen and Bertie from the spider web, then come home. Okay?"

He nodded, looking frightened—there would surely be some punishment today. He had not thought there would be—they had gone so unnoticed these last couple of days.

Maggie cupped her hand over his head and leaned toward him. "When you're back in the house, go to the black box with my things. Inside, you'll find a pack of chewing gum that you can share. Make sure Bertie doesn't swallow his."

Together the two scampered off to gather their siblings. She pulled the door closed behind her, not sure of this instinct except that she did not want Phillip to find it open and make accusations of the little ones when she was not there to defend them. She ducked her head as she descended the stairs, gritting her teeth when the crickets bounced erratically along the walls. On the wooden slats were muddy footprints, too large to belong to the children. They were her father's, possibly, a puzzle since their own yard had grown dry in the sun. Once on the dusty concrete floor, she looked around the cellar. The shelves were empty, but in the shadows beneath the stairs was a long tie, coiled in the dust. She picked it up carefully and shook it off. The maroon fabric was smudged, but she recognized the tie as one in her father's regular rotation. He had packed some things. She understood now why she'd not been awakened by her father's late arrival home the night before or by his exit later. He had been so cautious and yet also careless, not just now but beginning some time ago. She felt the strange ache of questions about how long he would be gone, why he had left, and whether he would be back for her. Tomorrow he was to take her to the church in the city, but without evidence that he would return, Maggie could not quite envision it.

She crossed the floor to the far back corner, where there was a small door. It stood open now, but she could not hear any voices. If even at nineteen she was unnerved by this venture into the dark, her siblings must be putting on brave faces for one another. As her eyes adjusted, a passage became visible, extending away from the pale glow of the naked bulb in the cellar. It was built sturdily of stone and was dry, and though life even now squirmed and rooted in the heavy weight of soil above, nothing grew or breathed here. She stepped through the doorway, where the temperature seemingly dropped.

Within a few moments' progress down the passage, the darkness completely surrounded her. Feeling her way along the tunnel that was as narrow as a casket, she remembered an old story she'd once heard in which a mother awoke in the middle of the night screaming and sobbing, insisting to her husband and son that the daughter they'd buried the day before was in fact alive—they had been wrong to bury her. She begged them to go to the cemetery and dig up the body, but the men were frightened by the mother's hysteria and reasonable in their own grief: they told her to go back to sleep. The next morning, when the mother still insisted that they go dig up the girl, the two men, hearts heavy, agreed to do so—what else, after all, could they do to satisfy her? There was no clever girl nor a friendly horse in this burial story, and the mother hadn't gone out and dug up the body herself, as she should have done. For this reason, the family opened the casket to find the girl's fingertips and calico dress covered in blood, her fingernails ripped to shreds. On her frozen features was an expression of deepest horror: she had awakened from her coma only to be suffocated by the earth.

Like that girl, Maggie felt she might not ever reach those in the house above her, a family that would scatter when the corpse among them was revealed. She might scream as long as she wanted, or dig through the earth with her fingertips, but they would ignore her, doubtful about what it was they were hearing, unsure of whether her absence should be discussed, disinclined to introduce an upsetting topic or ask any questions. After a few more moments, however, she reached the door at the other end, smaller than the doors of the house. Once through, she was disoriented until she recognized that she was behind the plywood wall of the basement, light coming in through the cracks in the foundation. She saw the base of a wooden staircase a few feet away and quickly crossed the concrete floor to reach it, feeling as though she must hurry.

Climbing the stairs, she passed through an open door and entered the house, making a sharp turn on a landing that was some place near the kitchen, perhaps. Here the narrow steps became plaster, the smooth white walls dimly lit by an open door above. The floors creaked softly and she could picture Warren, sitting even now at his desk, knowing all along where the cat had disappeared to yesterday. He must have known, too, the sound of footsteps on the stairs, and much more besides. Yet he was waiting now for what was done to be done, as he had been waiting these many years. She felt a wave of revulsion for his passivity, followed by a piercing pity: he had been put on watch long ago and never been relieved.

Maggie understood that at the top of the stairs, she would find the room her mother sat weeping in the night before. She could hear the whispers of her two siblings now, followed by an unfamiliar voice that caused her pulse to suddenly race forward. She climbed more quietly, unsure why except from the knowledge that there were too many people and too much activity in this place that had been hidden for so long. She did not know whether she would reprimand Agnes and Douglas or speak to them sweetly, unsure of what the discovery of the room meant in their minds except that their father kept secrets, which everyone had already known for quite some time.

When she reached the top, she stared through a half-opened door at a glimpse of dusty wooden floor beyond. The voices had grown quiet, and so when she stepped into the room she expected to see brother and sister and neighbor side-by-side facing her, anticipating the coming reproach, looking young and sheepish, abashed or arrogant. Instead, Douglas stood in the middle of a pile of torn pages, his mouth open, staring at a wad of paper in his hands. On the bare single bed pushed against the wall, Agnes lay on her back beneath the neighbor boy, who had his palms pressed against her breasts and who was breathing loudly very close to her face. They were both fully clothed. He turned his head when he heard Maggie's boot hit the floor, brown locks shielding his eyes. Her sister tried to see around him but could not.

In the moment before she spoke, Maggie did not see the neighbor boy at all, but another boy, the receptionist's son, not the one who had died (she was bumping along, riding on his shoulder, bumping along, riding in the wheel barrow), but his brother, the one who lived far away now and no longer came to visit. She heard again her mother's whisper on the stairwell of the receptionist's house as they discussed what to do and decided—what?—to do what? One mother confided in the other, warning but not condemning, because together they knew there was only so much that could be done about moments like these, when in leaving the Halloween party the wheel barrow had been pulled to one side of the trail so that the older brother could reach beneath the stretchy tube of the mermaid costume to grope there among the smooth bare folds as the younger brother watched. Two brothers, four and five years older than she, hovered over her in the wheelbarrow, a moment that did not connect in time to any other moment, as in a dream, without a real beginning or end, and which receded again just as she heard her voice, deep and trembling, say, "Get off her, you bastard."

The neighbor boy was gone in moments. His retreat was loud, full of fear. Douglas' gaze reverted to the floor. Noticing again the torn paper there, he settled instead for looking toward the window.

Maggie ignored him, crossing the room to sit beside Agnes, who had sat up on the bed, tears running down her face. Maggie wrapped her arms around her younger sister.

"He told me to," Agnes whispered into Maggie's neck. "I didn't know what to do."

"I know," Maggie said, "It's not your fault."

The sun shone fully into the room, and as she held her sister closely, Maggie took into account the details—books scattered across the floor, pages ripped, the smashed up remains of colored glass like the pile outside of Mamie's house. A large flashlight on the floor had presumably been used to break the glass. Maggie understood without knowing quite how that the flashlight had at some time sent light through the river cane down to Mamie's house, just as the receptionist had used the balloons to signal to her brother. She knew, too, that a servant had once lived in this room, paid to climb the stairs to wait upon the man in the master bedroom, who was in need, and she saw that her father had been that servant, waiting on the needs of the man in the master bedroom that no one else could satisfy.

CHAPTER FOURTEEN

Douglas knew he would never be able to forget the torn photographs crumpled in his hand or piled in a heap at his feet, images he'd lingered over in an effort to avoid the trouble his friend began creating as soon as they entered the tunnel and that suddenly seemed beyond Douglas' ability to name or alter. Or was it that the photographs themselves had drained all ability to act? Seeing Maggie cross the room disrupted this paralysis, and he thought to feel liberated—someone had intervened—but what she said and did confirmed his failure, that he had somehow invited in some evil and then been powerless to banish it again.

"The same thing happened to me once," Maggie now said to Agnes, and by the uncertainty in her voice Douglas knew she wasn't sure whether saying so would help or harm. He felt his own responsibility double, but she was not speaking to him.

Agnes looked up. "Really?"

Maggie nodded, "When I was your age. An older boy. He also lived nearby." She spoke as if testing each word.

Douglas heard his mother bumping around in her room, an unexpected reminder that this place connected to other places, and that time still moved in the realm beyond. Maggie and Agnes heard, too, and were looking toward the door that must lead to the bathroom, expecting her to enter at any moment. Douglas finally let the paper fall from his hands and half-turned to the staircase door, thinking that Maggie would want him to go back the way he'd come. They would close up the room and behave as if none of them had ever been here for the sake of their mother's fragile psyche, for the sake of all of their shame. After all, he had heard the wailing the night before better than anyone else, and he understood without the haze or confusion of dreams that his father's crying had sometime later followed his mother's.

Instead, Maggie looked at him and said, "Go get Mother." She spoke gently, but when he looked toward the door he knew would lead to his parents' bedroom, he was unable to imagine doing such a thing. "You'll have to tell her what happened."

He shook his head, face contorted in the effort not to cry.

"You're going to have to go to your friend's house," she said, and paused, letting him absorb this idea. "You and mother. You'll have to tell his mother that her son touched your sister where he should have not touched her." She glanced at Agnes, who was calmly looking back at her, tears dried, then continued. "She'll be angry, probably. Not at him but at you. You'll have to repeat yourself. Say, 'Your son touched my sister where he should not have touched her, and he is no longer welcome at our house.' Do you understand?"

Douglas felt frozen to the spot.

"Mother will go with you. But you were here, and so you are the one who needs to say these things." She paused. "You'll feel better, after, and so will Agnes."

Douglas glanced at Agnes but she was staring at the floor, her head resting on Maggie's shoulder. He took a few hesitant steps through the crumpled paper. At the smooth surface of the door he stopped, unsure of how to open it, hoping to find it locked. He leaned against it, feeling his sore back and shoulder muscles. They were to be their own reward, he saw now. He could not refer to them offhand after receiving a compliment from his father about the yard work that might not ever come. Douglas had bragged to Sean about how sore he was, and his friend said that was nothing compared to how he felt after loading wood all day; he'd told Phillip, and Phillip told him that if he ran sixteen miles in one day he'd know what sore was. But then, Douglas also knew that telling his father might not have left him with any greater satisfaction. His father might not have heard, might have seemed irked by the thinly veiled bragging, might have dismissed him with a command to shear the hedges closer next time. And so Douglas saw that any efforts he made he must make for himself, never looking for approval from others. He pushed the door one more time, and it gave way.

The bathroom door on the other side was open, revealing their mother sitting on the bed in her rose-colored dress with her long hair brushed. She was facing the bathroom as if expecting them and ready to make the next move, whatever that might be. Her eyes were swollen but her expression serene, without any question about what the children were doing there—they had heard the commotion, they had come to investigate, they had discovered things she could not keep from them. Douglas would have to tell her that though this was true, other things were true, too, but he would not explain until they were walking to see Sean's mother, away from the house and in motion. Still, though he did not know how he was to bear the telling, he also sensed that within these last few moments existed a portion of a story that he would have to share again and again, even though he had no one to tell it to, and no practice in the art of telling.

When Douglas approached the bed, mouth open but unable to speak, his mother reached out to fold him in one arm. With the other, she held out an old worn laundry bag for Maggie to take. Douglas buried his face against his mother's shoulder, and for a moment did not visualize the photographs or his sister submitting to another's commands, but simply smelled the baby powder she sometimes combed through her hair. When he opened his eyes again, his mother was holding Agnes with her other arm, and Maggie was disappearing back through the bathroom.

Maggie was glad to leave them for a moment to perform this duty. In the little room, she put the paper scraps into the bag first, intending to cushion the glass. She knew that this was what their mother would have done, and Maggie felt a closeness with her at that moment, the practical orientation to tasks that daughter had learned from mother at a time when the mother was more proficient. She did not pause over the scraps of paper as her mother and brother had done, nor did she close her eyes to the shades of black and white that, reassembled, would tell so little about what really mattered for their father. After some small exchange of words, her mother and brother and sister fell silent, but this interlude would not last long, the awkwardness quickly returning as a strange byproduct of being soothed back into an awareness of time. Downstairs, too, the other children would be uneasy, and she hoped Warren would intervene.

She stuffed an old jumpsuit into the bag, then crossed the room to pick up chunks of glass from beneath the window, feeling rejuvenated by ordinary movement, as if all complications could be resolved by routine chores. When she stood, ready to tie off the bag, she saw the sweep of valley below her, with neighbors fanning out like an apron beneath the house. Here, just a few feet away from her old window, she could see the tiniest tip of Mamie's chimney and a flash of tin roof from her grandparents' farmhouse. Somewhere between the two, she could guess where wood smoke would drift above her grandmother's cottage in the winter. Her neighbors and kin had been there all along, and she hadn't known it. These last three days she'd felt she owed them something—some form of payment or an explanation for her family's long seclusion—when in fact her neighbors owed something to her and to her siblings, whom they had both sacrificed and protected.

Her mother was standing as Maggie reentered the bedroom carrying the bag. The four of them passed through the children's room, leaving all of the doors open behind them. In a little while, Maggie would return to the passage to lock the cellar door as well as the two basement doors, but the other doors she would leave open, eventually even prying back the false wall at the far end of the pantry, hoping in the meantime that Lula would run in a loop around the house that would help them all grow accustomed to the new space, allowing the taint of secrecy to fade—it would not do to have the room closed off and empty, haunting them with possibilities while they pretended it did not exist. Soon they would all warm to the place, and someone would want to use it.

In the living room, they found the four littlest ones crowded onto the couch, chewing their gum with such concentration that they'd fallen silent. Their eyes grew wide as their siblings and mother entered—where then had they come from? Maggie couldn't help but laugh at their surprise. She laughed, too, because the sweetness of the gum was fleeting, and she could tell that they chewed hard now because they were not yet willing to admit that such a rare treat had already expired.

Thinking so gave her an idea, just as Warren stepped out of his room tentatively, as if not sure whether he was invited. She turned to him and said, "I'd like you to do an errand." Warren said nothing. "We're all in need of a distraction, and since cake might do the trick, perhaps you could get a bit of grocery money from the kitchen." She glanced at their mother for permission as she said this, but somehow they all understood that their mother would not forbid them the cake. "The boys can tell you how to get to Mamie's house if you've forgotten."

"I know the way."

Quinn jumped up from the couch and said breathlessly, "A cake!" The last fretful hour had been so long, not knowing what was happening and whether the event would cause rupture or recovery. "What kind of cake would you like, Mother?"

She stared at Quinn for one long moment. "Cake?" she said, and they all saw that she was trying to remember. They would have eaten anything for her at that moment—carrot cake with walnuts, chocolate cake moistened with tomatoes, pineapple upside-down cake. "Poppy seed cake," she finally said, "with lemon glaze." She spoke with conviction, and the children remained still, wondering what such a cake might taste like. "She will have the recipe." She paused, then said to the children, "Douglas and I are going to buy seeds for the garden. Be good for Maggie while we're gone."

They turned to leave through the kitchen, followed by Warren. In the living room, Agnes picked up Bertie and made a place for herself on the couch with the others, with Bertie settling back on her lap. "Were you scared, Agnes?" Ellen asked, taking her sister's hand. "Was it very dark?"

Agnes nodded, and the children sat in awe of a darkness that had the power to subdue their older sister. Maggie took the laundry bag to the pantry garbage can, listening to their gentle chatter. Her siblings would not arrive at the most important questions directly. They would not ask where the passage led nor why the neighbor boy disappeared suddenly like a banished demon. Not yet.

When she returned, Maggie took the rocking chair by the wood stove, away from the children, who for the moment did not need her.

"I think a cave cricket hopped on my head," Edwin said, reaching across Ellen to tweak Bertie's hair.

"Hey now!" Bertie said. He made his fingers look like a spider, hopping across all of their knees.

Maggie turned her attention from them as Phillip came through the kitchen door, sweaty from a long run. He seemed bewildered to find Maggie sitting beside the stove. When he came toward her, the children looked up but did not cease playing.

"I passed Mother on my way home," he said. "She said she and Douglas were on their way to the hardware store." His statement was intended to be a question. He wanted to understand why the routine had changed today, and like the children, did not want to ask directly, lest he should expose some ignorance of his own.

"Yes, that's true," Maggie said. She suddenly felt anger welling within her—the desire to avenge some series of disappointments she could only partly catalogue. Her brother seemed an appropriate vessel for blame, stumbling now into their intimate gathering with an apparent innocence that she would rob him of if she could.

She stood and motioned him to sit with her at the dining room table, out of earshot of the children chattering on the couch. Phillip followed her but did not sit, as she did, on the long bench. He waited in dread for what she would say, for he saw that it was to be no small thing.

"I'd like you to go to our neighbor's house and tell her we're keeping Lula."

He was stunned. "For how long?"

"For good," Maggie said.

"She won't—" Phillip stopped, afraid he'd given himself away. "Why would she give us her cat?"

Maggie stared at him, waiting for him to understand—which he quickly did—that she knew he was visiting Jocelyn that morning, and that she saw some shame in it, some threat to the order of things. She must have heard him or seen him or perhaps Jocelyn herself had told her; however little Phillip knew about Jocelyn he recognized she might do such a thing for her own reasons. Maggie would not care about the pleasure or fear that each visit evoked for him, and he felt, with some despair, that no one else here would care, either—not his father or mother or his older brother. Not that he needed his private joys to matter to them. Not that he could ask for that kind of interest from his family, any more than he could ask for help when the source of that joy vanished, as surely it soon would, leaving him marooned.

Phillip glanced at the children, who had found Quinn's vocabulary cards between the cushions of the couch and were now spreading them across their knees, filling in the blanks to make silly sentences, as Maggie had long ago taught them to do. He leaned closer to Maggie. "When are you leaving?" he hissed. He resented his sister's ongoing presence, her uncertain departure. He wanted to believe it was possible to leave, and when he saw her again sometime later, wanted to see something about her that would show him how to go himself. Yet she was still here, rocking in the chair, giving orders after a short hiatus. And though he understood that she was not supposed to leave until tomorrow, and that she could not leave without a ride from their father, nothing about these past three days suggested she had ever been preparing to leave at all. He'd wanted to see her piecing together a new dress at the dining room table, mending her stockings, studying a map, reading books on childcare, whatever it was that might suggest she was arranging her departure, rather than wandering the countryside discovering things she ought not to discover. And now Maggie was again in the center of things, pulled from the margins and into the fray of whatever it was that had disrupted this morning's schedule, so that she was once more managing and directing and delegating. Phillip was afraid for her, and for himself.

She let his question about her leaving sit, then she turned to him, smiling sadly, and said, "But don't you know? Our father is gone."

He stared at her, wondering at her directness, her tone of finality. She seemed an authority on knowledge that for him was only just surfacing, with few facts or points of reference.

He shivered with the cold sweat on his back. "And so you're to take his place?"

Maggie paled. She had been warned—by the witch, by her father, by Warren, by the fat lady, by her grandmother. She could have stayed close to home while she waited to leave, abiding by the rules and keeping to herself.

Phillip watched as she twisted her hands and looked toward the children, thinking, he knew, about which ones would be okay without her, and which ones would not, a belated consideration, surely. He did not know by what standards she might judge, or why their father's absence from the house would create more, rather than fewer, reasons to stay.

"And don't you know," she said, her tone fierce, as if she was determined to tell him some ugly truth about himself, "that we have grandparents?" She turned to face him again, eyes narrowed. "A grandmother who lives in a cottage in the woods, who Mother stopped speaking to long ago? Grandparents who live in a farmhouse beyond the cornfield, who stopped speaking to Father long ago?"

He did not know, and sat down beside her finally, intent that the children should not hear. She lowered her voice, saying, "And don't you know that Quinn is right, that the woods are filled with tramps—with neighbor boys who prey upon children, just as the fat lady's companion does, just as the receptionist does?" He flinched, but she was not finished, "And don't you know," she breathed, "that our father loves men?"

Without understanding all that she said, Phillip felt the truth take shape within him. He did not feel like speaking, so he shook his head to keep her from becoming more hostile. For he could see that she was angry at him for somehow missing all of this, for not knowing about any of it. "I didn't know," he whispered.

Maggie saw her brother's eyes fill, not so much from sadness, she thought, but from the force of his confusion. She straightened, clearing her throat, because she saw that the children had grown quiet and were watching them. In a moment, she would send them out to gather mint from the overgrown garden so they could make tea. They would stay together through the long afternoon as people did who were in mourning, sharing food and a spring fire and listening to their mother tell stories about themselves that they had forgotten—a wake with hope of renewal in the morning. They would close their eyes and taste the sweet citrus of the cake on their tongues, would breathe the lemon-soaked air around them as their mother's words began to break the long spell of silence.

But no matter how good the cake tasted, when night fell the children would begin waiting and not waiting, understanding that their father would not likely be home that day or perhaps any of the next, not because they had guessed as much by listening to the sounds of the house, but because Maggie would tell them. She would tell them if their mother did not. She would give the children time to understand, hoping their mother would offer the reasons that she could and answer the questions that would come, as all of their questions did, indirectly and with hesitation. They would have to be patient with one another as they felt their way along this new terrain, harbored in unknown territory where language might be allowed, unable to move freely until fluent. For they had all begun a struggle over what to say and what not to say, when to say it and in what way and to whom. Maggie knew they would do so badly and in spite of themselves, hoping others would listen past the details for the origin of stories, occurring once and repeatedly across the limitless span of time.

Acknowledgments

The author wishes to acknowledge the following print and audio texts, portions of which are incorporated as loosely paraphrased anecdotes in the novel. They are listed in the order in which they appear:

Herzog, Werner. *Conquest of the Useless: Reflections from the Making of Fitzcarraldo*. New York: Ecco, 2010. Rpt. in *Harper's Magazine* as "The Jungle is Obscene," June 2009. Print.

Spofford, Harriet Prescott. "Circumstance." *Atlantic Monthly* May 1860. Rpt. in *The Norton Anthology of American Literature* 1820-1865. Vol. B. Ed. Hershel Parker and Arnold Krupat. 6th ed. New York: W.W. Norton & Company, 2003. 2588-2597. Print.

Connie Regan-Blake. "Two White Horses." *Chilling Ghost Stories*. Asheville, NC: StoryWindow Productions, 1999. CD.

Connie Regan-Blake and Barbara Freeman. "Calico Coffin." *The Chillers*. Asheville, NC: Mama T Artists, 1983. Audiocassette.

AUTHOR

PHOTOGRAPH BY LISA MORRIS

Elizabeth Gentry received the 2012 Madeleine P. Plonsker Emerging Writer's Residency Prize for *Housebound*. Originally from Asheville, North Carolina, she lives in Knoxville, Tennessee, where she works as Writing Specialist for the University of Tennessee College of Law and teaches for the University English Department. She received a MFA in fiction writing from the University of North Carolina at Greensboro.